"Finally, a discussion about art that I understand."
	- Abigail Critchley Davis

"This book has left me more confused about art than ever."
	- Emily Trumbull Ryan

"Beauty is in the depth of the wallet."
	- Morris Quint

"How much unaffordable art does the world need?"
	- The Author's Mother

Copyright © Michael Reidy 2022

All rights reserved

Cover photographs by Victor Ochando and the author.
Cover design by Bespoke Designs, Yelverton, Devonshire.

ISBN: 9798402695153

Circle of Vanity

a novel by

Michael Reidy

Lattimer & Co.

PHILADELPHIA & PARIS

2022

For Steph

*a figurative painter extraordinaire who makes
Edinburgh more colourful*

"The public are rather tiresomely fascinated by forgery, more so, I'm afraid, they are by the real thing."

Sir Anthony Blunt
in *A Question of Attribution*

vi

Foreword

In August 2021, the BBC broadcast an episode of its popular series *Fake or Fortune* that examined the authenticity of a painting attributed to "the circle of Jean-Léon Gérôme."

Episode 2 of Series 9 traced the sale of the painting from when it was sold as a genuine Gérôme at the Shickman Gallery in New York in 1971, to its sale in 1978 at Christie's, London, again as a genuine Gérôme.

However, when it was bought in 1999 at Christie's in New York, something had happened, and it was listed as "circle of Gérôme," drastically reducing its value. In the intervening years, the *Catalogue Raisonée* for Gérôme had been published which had downgraded the painting to its "circle of" status. The downgrading was based purely on the opinion of one man, but later backed by others.

Ultimately, following the programme's investigation, the painting was restored to its "by Gérôme" status, elevating its value from a thousand pounds to several hundred thousand.

While a satisfying story, viewers had also seen the fundamental canker at the heart of the art market, for as the painting's value plummeted and soared, not a single brushstroke had changed.

Prologue

After recording the complicated entry of the actress Ligeia Gordon into my life in *On the Edge of Dreams and Nightmares*, I thought my world would settle back into its uneventful routine.

I should have known better.

The lives of award-winning actresses are far more eventful than those of portrait painters – even award-winning ones. For those who have not yet read *On the Edge of Dreams and Nightmares*, I am a portrait painter.

"A painter of portraits" sounds pretentious for what I do. I am like the builder you call in to put on an extension: he discusses the project, quotes a price, uses his skill to do the work, and he goes away, leaving his work to be appreciated – or not. There's little more to it.

Usually.

Ligeia Gordon was the great exception. She commissioned me to paint her portrait, and, during the process, told me that we once had an encounter when she, as a fourteen-year-old, had come to visit her cousin who was at the same Cambridge college where I was a graduate student. Then, she was Sophie Gregg.

Based on that tenuous connection (and other events), she insinuated herself into my life.

We now both live – separately – in sets at Albany, that distinguished "boarding house" (as Dame Edith Evans called it) just off Piccadilly, and next to the Royal Academy of Art.

Our friendship is very close but chaste. For brevity, we tell people that we are cousins; that stops most awkward questions and speculations, but the truth is far more complicated and dark.

From there, my normal world extends to my studio in Southwark, my club in Mount Street Gardens, the Royal Academy, and Farm Street Church.

I do go further afield, but nothing compared to Ligeia who performs and films all over the world.

In this record, I will refer to her as Sophie unless the context demands the use of her stage name.

While my position in the art world was a reason I was drawn into the events of this story, it was the discipline of my earlier career that was initially sought.

Much good it did anyone.

Albany
January 2022

Circle of Vanity

Chapter I

A fter more than two years of enforced hibernation –
which saw the near total end to my portrait painting
– life returned to normal with the sort of zest that it
appeared to have done in the 1920s after the Spanish Flu
had passed.

Even though I am what I call "semi-retired," I still go
to my studio most days, and the number of sitters is
returning nearly to pre-retirement levels. At one point, I
began to wonder if there would be any room for them as
my studio was filling up with pictures. I had gone to my
studio daily as part of my allowed "exercise" though I was
stopped by the police on more than one occasion and
asked what I was doing walking down Piccadilly or
through Trafalgar Square.

I painted every day: from memory, and, occasionally,
from photographs, which I very seldom do. I also
experimented with different styles. Many I later scraped
down and re-primed the canvas. The net effect was that I
was running out of storage space.

However, the end of restrictions re-opened the various
outlets for my pictures and plying my trade returned to
normal.

What I did enjoy, perhaps even more, was the re-opening of my club in Mount Street Gardens, and the resumption of the company of old friends, food I didn't cook myself, and lively discussions.

One March evening, I went there for a drink and supper. Sophie was away visiting an old university friend in Lincolnshire so would not be expecting to be taken to dinner.

There was a large number of people that I hadn't seen for over a year, so catching up with them was usually pleasurable. On this particular evening, I found Sir John Hawsley checking his coat as I walked in.

We greeted each other with greater enthusiasm than usual, glad to see the other still alive. We exchanged pleasantries, our experiences of the past two years and our relative health before settling on our more usual topics of conversation.

Hawsley was chairman of Brooke & Sons, the largest auction house in London. Running a close second was Sibley & Hood, with Moorhouse & Co. in show position. Brooke, and Sibley & Hood were now part of international conglomerates or asset managers, but Moorhouse remained a private company. A much smaller business, it had no branches outside London and was as well-respected as the other two, by some, considerably more.

Hawsley joined me for dinner. He was interesting company and could be amusing, and although charming and affable, he was also one of the toughest businessmen I ever met. As for his knowledge of art, it was extensive, but he had no intuition for it. For him, it was the bottom-line all the way. A considerable mitigating factor was that he liked my work. I had painted him when he was forty. That gave us a nearly twenty-year acquaintance, if not friendship.

We had finished our meal and were idling over coffee and brandy when, having talked in generalities and art world gossip, he became serious.

"Did you read about the appearance of the Jan Steen about six months ago?" he asked.

I could tell it was not a casual question.

"The one at Gwilym Jones & Stottlemeyer?"

He nodded.

The name always made me chuckle, but such combinations were common in Patagonia. The Jan Steen Hawsley was referring to was completely unknown. When it reached the auction house in Buenos Aires, it attracted the attention of curators, experts and academics from around the world.

"Could they prove it was Nazi plunder?" I asked.

"It seems most likely," he replied, "but the problem is that it's not on any of the lists of plundered art. No one reported it stolen, nor does it have any of the tell-tale inventory labels of the Nazis, Fascists or Russians."

This was unusual as spoliated art was usually recorded, marked, and its details circulated around the world.

"The experts were virtually unanimous that it was by Steen," Hawsley said, "but, of course, would only publicly state that it was 'after Steen' or 'school of Steen.' Privately, they were convinced it was the real thing."

"Provenance?"

"Nothing. It was probably taken by or from some Dutchman who'd had it in his family for three hundred years."

He paused to sip his brandy.

"That's the real problem. More records were lost than anyone wants to admit," he added.

I knew this. Unless a work had been exhibited, exported or sold by an international dealer or auction house, records could be thin or non-existent. Local auctions in the nineteenth century had very basic information in their catalogues – if there was a catalogue at all. Who knows what escapes notice in house clearances and sales?

The notion that all important art is properly documented is a misconception. About two-thirds of it is, but the rest is inherited, given away or sold at car boot fairs and remain as anonymous as their owners. There are the occasional spectacular finds by someone who has a good eye or is just lucky.

These paintings are legitimate in every way: who gets the details of a young street artist? "Oh, my great aunt went to Italy when she was young and bought that. . . ." No one sees it as anything but a cheap tourist piece, and who knew that Modigliani painted bridges and fountains?

What this means is that very often, the spoliated pictures have much better provenance than those acquired more casually.

"The Steen passed through London in December. Moorhouse had it and invited the chosen to see and examine it *en route* to Amsterdam," he said. "I won't say they were nervous about it, but they wanted it to be seen by us so we couldn't disparage it in the course of its future history.

"While we couldn't test it, they let us look everywhere," he added.

"What did you make of it?"

"I took our expert on the period and our top technical chap. Moorhouse gave us a copy of the test results carried out in South America. We saw nothing at all that was suspect, and the conclusion was there was nothing to warrant further tests. *Nothing.* Just no damn *provenance.*"

"Did that surprise you?" I asked.

He shrugged.

5

"I don't know what we expected, but this was as right as anything I've seen, and I've seen some pretty dodgy stuff."

And sold it, I thought.

"A wonderful benefit for the art world," I said. "Where is it now?"

"It hasn't been announced, but the Rijksmuseum has it, pending a decision to acquire."

Hawsley knew he didn't need to caution me about telling anyone. The only people I'd be apt to tell would probably know already, and they would report that I couldn't keep my mouth shut. I'd kept it shut about more important things – and for longer – so, this wouldn't tempt me.

"I look forward to reading about it."

Hawsley looked grave and lowered his voice.

"It happened again," he said.

I stared at him, wondering what.

"Last month, an unknown Rembrandt showed up at Weisman & Rossi, in Los Angeles.

"As soon as Saul saw it, he called Bob Longman in our office there."

Hawsley looked around, but there was no one near us.

"Everyone from both houses thought it was genuine, but no one could find a reference. It's not in any sale catalogue, or on any museum list," he stopped. "*Do you know how unlikely that is? An* unknown *Rembrandt?*"

I sensed that direct questioning would yield less than the indirect approach.

"What's the subject?" I asked, thinking it might be a portrait that could be traced via the sitter.

"It's a seascape," he said, as if he hardly believed it himself. "It's another version of *The Storm on the Sea of Galilee.*"

Rembrandt's only known seascape was already remarkable and, when it was stolen from the Isabella Stuart Gardner Museum in 1990 in the largest art heist in history, it became almost as famous as *La Gioconda*.

"That sounds interesting," I said, feigning indifference. "Presumably, it's real."

Hawsley gave a deep sigh.

"Weisman & Rossi had it tested and it's coming to Europe for further testing."

"I bet the Yanks love that," I couldn't resist saying.

"I'm going to see it with the London team in Amsterdam," he resumed. "Of course, the Americans regard it as a courtesy, being confident that their experts have handled it."

The arrogant disdain could not be disguised.

"Do you know how improbable it is that two totally unknown Old Master paintings surface within six months of each other?" he asked, gravely. "Neither with any known history and no real *provenance*."

"Who owns the Rembrandt?"

Hawsley gave a laugh of frustrated disbelief.

"It was brought in by the widow of someone who had worked for MGM or Twentieth Century. When her husband died, he left her with a houseful of stuff and this was there," he said. "She claims not to have known anything about it; that he had never talked about it, and gather it had been a bit of decoration from a film set. Indeed, it appears to have been."

I couldn't contain my laughter. The story and Hawsley's discomfiture were equally amusing. Hawsley, of course, saw it as no laughing matter.

"I guess this is another one the Rijksmuseum will have to pony up for," I said. "What a terrific story!"

Hawsley shook his head.

"I don't like it. One is bad enough, but *two* – and one of them so close to the most famous missing picture in the world! Someone is playing an elaborate trick."

"So, it's a fake?"

"Not that anyone's been able to prove so far," he replied, shortly. "They are exactly the same size, but this is landscape and the stolen one is portrait."

I laughed again to his growing annoyance.

"Are you sure it's not painted on top of the missing one?"

He considered this.

"It's been X-rayed," he said, then after a pause added: "There is something else that can be done."

"And that is?" I asked, then finished my brandy.

"Find out what's *really* going on," he said, then added, "And, that's why I'd like your help."

Chapter II

"What can *I* do?" I exclaimed, quietly. "I don't have the sort of expertise you need."

Hawsley raised his hand slightly.

"There are some wonderful art dealers, experts and technicians," he said, "but very few of them are objective thinkers. They – *we* – see what we expect to see. Our vision is too narrow – in spite of how much we protest.

"Quite simply, there is virtually no one like you in the art world."

He didn't give me time to protest.

"You were educated by the Jesuits," he said, revealing information I was unaware he had about me. "That gives you insight, logic and respect for evidence. You were also a naval officer. That demands an orderly mind.

"My mind is polluted: I can do nothing but believe that at least one of these paintings is a very clever fake, and probably both.

"I have read the reports and I will go to see them both in Amsterdam. It will be interesting to see if the Steen makes the same impression," he continued. "However, I know what I will see with the Rembrandt: I will see it as a fake. Everything I have read about it makes it seem too perfect. I know I am prejudiced – and so was everyone else who has seen it."

The conversation needed some reality.

"You are less prejudiced than most dealers," I said. "I'm not sure I'm any better – and I still don't see how I can be of any help."

Hawsley paused for so long that I thought he was going to change his mind.

"Look," he said, speaking with less caution and more humanity than before. "An unknown Picasso appears. It might be right, it might be a forgery: it doesn't matter. Picasso did so many pictures there are bound to be a few hundred strays.

"This is true of almost any nineteenth or twentieth century painter," he said. "One more or less is a bit of fun, a two-day scandal, and it's back to business as usual. Yes, some of us will have egg on our faces, and too often it serves us right."

I thought of John Myatt painting Monets using household emulsion from a hardware chain store and having them approved by experts.

There was also Tom Keating who used to paint a layer of gelatine over indifferent Victorian paintings of fruit or dead pheasants and painting a fake Samuel Palmer or Thomas Lawrence on the new surface. The gelatine base meant that the painting would dissolve down to the pheasants when cleaned. Keating was also known to paint, "This is a fake" on his canvases before painting a "valuable" work, knowing that it would show up under modern image analysis.

When Hawsley resumed speaking, I did my best to hide a smug smile.

"The truth is, your opinion is valuable because you never went to art school," he said, finally. "Your head isn't full of a lot of nonsense. You were trained as a mathematician."

I laughed and demurred, but he wasn't having any of it.

"Let me send you all the documents that I received about these pictures," he said, his mood lightening slightly. "Read them. There are some excellent photos, diagrams, and spreadsheets that a mathematician will easily understand. Damned if I do."

I very much doubted if that were true.

"If these are being manufactured, they are convincing on a scale we haven't seen before – " Hawsley continued, "but so is everything else: the canvas, the pigments, the ground. On the Steen, even the nails and tacks are right. The pollen tests haven't been completed."

I sat back. It was flattering to be enlisted as a scrutineer of sorts, but what real function my comments would serve was unclear.

"It could be coincidence," I said. "They could be real."

"Do you really believe that?" Hawsley challenged.

"I believe in innocence until guilt is proved," I replied. "And we haven't either painting."

Hawsley now sat back, closed his eyes, let his head fall back and took a deep breath. After a moment, he sat up and smiled.

"I knew you were the right choice."

ଛଠ

On Saturday morning, Sophie knocked on my door as I was finishing breakfast.

My Albany set had, for decades, been my sanctuary, visited by no one until her arrival in my life. Now, she considered it an extension to her own chambers, though she had no key and almost always knocked.

"I wanted to see you before you settled into your 'Scholarly Saturday'," she said. "You were still out when I got back last night."

Sophie sniffed the air before sitting on the sofa.

"Would you like some coffee?" I asked, taking the hint.

She smiled and nodded.

Although nearly sixty, with minimal makeup, she could pass for forty-nine – and frequently did in her films and on stage. She had the natural ease of a teenager that sailed between the coy and the serious.

Sophie's hair had been through a rainbow of colours since I first met her, depending on her current role, but it was naturally very dark. She was above average height, and when she wore heels, she could be about five-feet-eleven – more should the occasion demand.

Along with her presence, she retained her slim figure. Sometimes I worried about her as she was very good at camouflaging how thin she was. Still, her appetite always seemed to be good.

I returned from the kitchen with a mug of coffee for her.

"How was Lincolnshire?" I asked.

She made a face that showed mixed emotions.

"I went to see April Fisher – now April Gilliat. We were at Cambridge together. Her husband died last month," she said. "I waited until the usual flurry of visitors died down when I thought she'd still be feeling low, but about to begin her new life."

"Was it very bad?"

Sophie made another face. This was one of amusement.

"She seemed less upset at the loss of her husband than she did with having to handle all the farm paperwork," she said.

"Did he leave a mess?"

"No. Things were in good order and there is an established manager there, but it all needs monitoring and endless conversations with the accountants and the manager about subsidies, tax breaks, and crop rotation which she knows nothing about."

"How long had she been married?"

"Nearly forty years – I know; she should have learned something in that time," Sophie laughed. "Don't worry, I thought the same, but it would have been pointless to say anything. On top of that, the estate manager wants to retire in two years."

"Does she have any children?"

"A daughter, Marissa. She works as an estate agent in Horncastle," she replied.

"She'd be a great candidate for the job, then," I said.

"Not sure she's interested, though," Sophie said. "She's got this idea about excavating a ruin on the property. She's got a degree in Arch and Anth from Cambridge and hasn't been able to use it selling ticky-tacky little boxes or pebble-dashed semis."

"I bet she likes the money, though," I said.

"Mmm," Sophie nodded. "She's ambitious. Wants to get her FRICS membership, but I don't think money's an issue."

"She should have read Land Economy."

Sophie smiled and put down her coffee.

"I'm leaving for Yorkshire tomorrow afternoon," she said.

I nodded.

"Just a turnaround visit to London, then?"

Sophie was heading to Yorkshire – not for the Brontës this time, but for yet another television version of

Persuasion. I had never thought Yorkshire much like Somerset, but perhaps that's why I don't work for the BBC. Her part was only small, so she would be back the following Sunday if things went to schedule.

"You'll have a peaceful week," she said, still in her faux flirtatious mode. "You'll get a lot done."

I knew she was prodding me for a pseudo-romantic response. She didn't get one.

"I'll leave you to your Saturday," she said. "I know you are protective of that time."

"Come for supper," I said, knowing she was expecting the invitation.

"Don't work too hard," she laughed, and left.

My "Scholarly Saturday," as Sophie called it, was the day I didn't go to the studio, pay bills, schedule appointments or do anything but intellectually recharge.

I read the art magazines and the few scientific titles I still subscribed to. I'd write letters to old friends and have lunch at the club. This would be followed by conversation or reading the weekend *Financial Times*. Sometimes, I'd go up to Farm Street for the six o'clock Mass. Occasionally, I'd have coffee (drinks, more likely) with the Jesuits afterwards, but usually, I'd return home.

If Sophie didn't have a performance, opening or awards ceremony, she'd come for something to eat around eight.

Even after more than a decade, I knew she didn't feel wholly comfortable in my rooms, partly because of their Spartan look. I had nothing on any surfaces: no plants, , photographs, pieces of silver, ornaments and *objects d'art*, and partly because the few and formal pieces of furniture (a sofa, two end-tables, two armchairs and a coffee table) in a room twenty feet long. It was, according to Sophie, "Less than minimalist."

That wasn't entirely fair as nearly every square foot of wall space was covered with paintings, screen prints and antique etchings.

At the far end of the room was an antique oak drop leaf table with six ladder back chairs with rush seats. (You should have heard her when she discovered that I had no more than six of anything: plates, glasses, place-settings, and so on. What more do I need?)

However, the real source of unease was the metre square portrait of my late wife (my first portrait) hanging above the fireplace.

∽

Around mid-morning, I went down to check my post and found that Hawsley had dropped off two thick and heavy parcels that turned out to be photographs, reports, charts and chemical analyses of the two paintings discussed.

I had hoped that he'd only been flattering me for some other purpose and that I would not be drawn into questions of attribution.

Apart from a label with my name and address on each, there were the Roman numerals I and II on the respective parcels.

I opened the first and found a note from Hawsley on Brooke & Sons notepaper.

Dear Nigel,

Thank you for agreeing to have a look at the documents for the pictures we discussed. I know that your life is busy with painting the great and the good, entertaining Miss Gordon, and saying the rosary, but I would appreciate your comments – including your instinctive reactions – to the enclosed.

You cannot imagine the tremors that such sudden appearances of Old Masters cause in our febrile world.

These papers are copies, so feel free to scribble on them, but please return them when you have finished your evaluation.

The honest opinion of someone I have known for so long is very important in such matters.

Best,
John

Whether Hawsley's confidence was justified, I couldn't say, but I looked through the material to see what was there and began reading after lunch.

I moved to the dining table where I could spread out all the photographs and build a complete understanding of the painting. I fetched my LED torch and my head magnifying glasses to get a closer look. The images had been printed on a matt paper at a fairly high resolution so seeing brush strokes was possible in many places.

While I could see nothing obviously amiss, it was little like seeing the real thing. My overall impression was favourable. It was consistent with the period and the Steens I knew, but that wouldn't help Hawsley. He wanted me to look at the data – and there were pages of it.

Gwilym Jones & Stottlemeyer had done an excellent job in presenting the material. The results of each test were produced in the same format, so I didn't have to figure out how to read each section. This was also true of the commentaries. It was obvious that the forensic scientists were working from the same brief. Each started with an overall description of what their tests were designed to show. Next, they explained what parts of the picture they were studying: the canvas, the tacks, the ground, the dust, the wood and construction of the stretcher, the varnish, and the colours and pigments.

The chemical data in these last categories were made easier to understand as they included test results from a known Steen thought to be of the same period for comparison. The charts were supplemented by tables that listed the colours and showed whether they were present in the known paintings.

Finally, each set of tests had a conclusion stating whether the findings were consistent with the period and artist.

The conservator's report commented on each of the test reports and restated what he thought were the most indicative factors as well as adding his own expert opinion. For example, he noted that the canvas hadn't been lined or even repaired, suggesting that it had not been moved much and had probably hung for very long periods in the same place. (The pollen tests might indicate where.)

The summary went on for about eight pages with a comment on the subject of the painting, its size, the nature of the interior space and furnishings, the three figures and their dress and jewellery, the instruments they played, the light and the overall effect.

The final judgement was, I thought, well phrased: "While the emergence of a wholly unknown painting by an Old Master is extremely rare, we see nothing in its physical structure, condition, composition or execution to indicate that it is anything other than what it appears to be: an interior scene of three people playing period instruments by Jan Steen, dated 1660."

I gathered the typed sheets, but spread the photographs out again until they nearly covered the table. Before starting the second inspection, I saw that it was time for a gin and tonic.

I put my magnifying headset back on and took a critical look at the composition. I looked at the detail photos of the figures, hands and faces one more time before gathering them and putting them in the envelope. I then put it in the bottom drawer of the *escritoire* in my small study.

I took envelope II over to my armchair with my drink and looked through the photographs. There was a very slight flicker somewhere at the back of my brain which I noted but could not identify. I put it down to seeing an unfamiliar version of a familiar painting.

I moved to the sofa where I could put pages either side of me and on the coffee table as I read the scientific reports and commentaries, and flipped back and forth between them.

Compared to the report on the Steen, the Americans' report on the Rembrandt was a collection of different reports. No attempt had been made to unify the presentations, charts or tables so comparing like with like was impossible. Weisman & Rossi had given no baseline of comparable analyses of other Rembrandt works. The images were very good, however, and I was lost in the pattern of waves when there was a knock, and my door opened.

"Are you indecent?" Sophie asked.

Chapter III

While I didn't make panic-stricken moves to hide the pictures and files, I did deliberately turn them face down and put them back into the large folder.

"Sorry," she said, backing away. "More paintings of naked women?"

"Alas, no. Brooke & Sons asked me to review the documentation of a picture that might be coming up for auction."

"May I see?"

"Not yet," I said. "Once I've made up my mind, I'll show you."

From both my days with the Royal Navy and the Jesuits, I had learned that the best ruse is one that is ninety-five per cent truth. Sophie would not push or rummage. When needed, she'd respect my privacy and was very protective of her own.

Leaving the folder on the sofa, I rose to fetch a bottle of wine and glasses. I opened the bottle and poured her a glass. Before sitting down again, I collected the envelope and put it in my desk with the other one.

"When I met John Hawsley at the club the other day, he told me about the picture and asked if I'd have a look over the documentation," I said, moving back to my chair.

"Surely Brooke has hundreds of people who can do that better than you," Sophie said.

"Indeed. There is something John is uneasy about, but he wouldn't tell me what. I have to discover it," I said.

My Jesuit schooling would make me replay this conversation over in my head a number of times, but I considered it the preservation of a confidence extended to a friend. There was nothing criminal – yet – so, the slight deception was within an acceptable range.

"I expect you want to be fed, too," I said, raising my glass.

"It depends. Are you making anything good?"

"Just normal Saturday night fare," I said. "I was planning to make some spaghetti."

"Perfect," she said, snuggling into the corner of the sofa and pulling up her feet.

"I felt I had to be on my best behaviour at April's," Sophie said. "Oh, April was fine, but she had an endless string of people coming by, mostly just to deliver or collect something, and although she introduced me as Sophie, everyone seemed to know who I was."

I laughed.

"And do you not think that's why they came by?" I asked.

Her eyes widened. The thought appeared not to have occurred to her before.

"Do you really think so?" she asked. "Well, they must have thought me extremely dull."

She followed me to my small kitchen – what the Americans used to call a "Pullman kitchen" – and stood in the doorway and watched me cook.

From my limited ingredients, repertoire and space, I made a *spaghetti meridionale.* It just means "southern," but it's what the restaurant called it when I first had it. It's just a simple tomato sauce with bacon, black olive halves and raisins (currents or sultanas). I suspect, like *spaghetti puttanesca*, it was made from whatever could be found in the kitchen. However, the combination of salt, bitter and sweet in a decent sauce is just different enough to make it presentable.

Sophie's question about April's friends was not affectation: when she was Sophie, she was Sophie. In many ways, her attitude to being an actress was the same as mine towards being a painter: it was a job.

She could, of course, switch on the Ligeia Gordon persona when circumstances demanded, but when she walked down the street, took the Underground, shopped at Waitrose (or Aldi), she was Sophie Gregg.

I'd often wondered about the carapace that was Ligeia Gordon. Was it a reaction to her childhood abuse, or simply a way of keeping her personal and professional lives separated.

"My glass is empty," she said, waving it.

She had been talking more about April Fisher Gilliat, her pre-Tudor house, Bickering Place, and slightly scary daughter, Marissa.

"And so it shall remain until we're ready to eat."

She pouted, then laughed.

"Who will look after me in Yorkshire?"

Comments like that were best ignored

"Would you like to light the candles?"

She did and also quickly set out the cutlery, placemats and napkins. She always set our places at opposite ends of the table.

"In real life, actresses are meant to be seen at a distance," she said one evening when I suggested that we didn't need the *Citizen Kane* distance between ourselves, especially since it meant I had to stand up to retrieve the wine, which invariably found its place near her.

I made the final preparations, cut a loaf of French bread and served (remembering to top up her glass). Sophie indulged my habit of saying grace (*Benedictus, benedicat. . .*) and followed *Amen* with *bon appetitfun*.

On this occasion, she only paused for a short drink after our ritual before returning to talking about April and Bickering Place.

"There are a few pieces of nice furniture and a lot of tat. Same for the pictures and other décor. I sometimes wonder at my friends' taste."

"Yours being impeccable."

"Just like yours," she returned, glancing around the nearly empty room.

"What did April read at Cambridge?"

"French."

"Did she do anything with it?"

"She went shopping in Paris a few times."

She paused and tapped her glass on the table until I refilled it.

"Oh, she did well enough," Sophie continued. "She got a respectable 2.1 – and managed to have a *very* good time, too. Nothing too scandalous. Cambridge was remarkably quiet when we were there. The big protests were over, and the hippies had got jobs in the City."

"It takes a lot to overcome seven hundred years of inertia," I said.

"April isn't as much fun as she was. She grew up and grew dull – like most of my friends," Sophie reflected. "Quite a few see me as some sort of eccentric."

"I can't think why."

This earned me a dirty look.

"It's because you still think young," I added. "And, you haven't had time to grow up."

❧

Over coffee, Sophie asked if my work for Brooke would divert me from getting on with my "real work" as she called it.

I hoped not as I was still clearing the studio. Some pictures could go to the Royal Academy, others to the Royal Society of Portrait Painters. The odd gallery had contacted me for pictures, but I was more interested in finishing those whose composition had been interrupted. I'd continue to try to contact the sitters and companies and institutions that had commissioned them – and hoped they were still in business or alive.

I could tell Sophie was curious about what I was doing for Brooke & Sons. She didn't ask directly but began several conversations aimed at fishing for a clue. It wasn't often that I knew something she didn't, but I hoped I'd be able to tell her more on her return from Yorkshire.

Although only friends, the same sort of silence slowly fell over us as experienced by loved ones about to part. I think this was something that Sophie was both more and less aware of than I.

I had had a number of girlfriends before marrying Vera, and while her loss was a deadening experience, at least I knew the normal emotional patterns of couples, which Sophie did not. Her behaviour in those circum-stances was based on what she'd read or performed – most convincingly – in plays and films.

We overcame the silence with a debate about the merits of an old TV series that we'd both watched. While not a particularly weighty subject, our differing opinions on the quality of the story, acting and direction was amusing. As an actress, she saw things from a completely different perspective which could be fascinating.

"You're so easily taken in by a pretty face and a bit of mystery!" she exclaimed.

"Of course, I am!" I retorted. "That's why that trope has been successful since before Shakespeare!"

When we stopped laughing, Sophie asked:

"Do you really think she's attractive?"

This is always a dangerous question for any man to be asked by a woman. Age doesn't matter. Whatever the answer, it's wrong, and it only goes to prove – yet again – that what men and women find attractive in each other is unpredictable, unknowable and irrational.

"I think the character she's playing is attractive though not particularly nice," I said with, I hoped, enough equivocation to keep me safe.

Sophie stared at me.

"Hmm."

She thought a bit more.

"Nicely sidestepped," she conceded.

"I gather the actress is someone you know."

"Oh, yes," she said. "I auditioned for that part."

Chapter IV

After Sophie left, I thought more about how to handle the research Hawsley had given me. I had decided that the best I could do was look for holes in the logic, gaps in the argument, or anomalies in scientific results. It would be impossible to judge the pictures without seeing them (though many experts did).

My late wife had been a chemist while I had been a mathematician. We picked up a good deal of the other's basic knowledge along with the appropriate methods. Though it had been many decades, I was surprised how easily it came back to me.

I returned to the photographs of the Jan Steen. There was an excellent range of them from precise full images to a selection of highly magnified small details printed at high resolution. Individual brush strokes could be seen.

Next followed what provenance was known, which wasn't much. The frame was not original, nor the stretcher. While both could be indicators of forgery, they were not proof, but did support the opinion, expressed by several of the "experts" that it could be indicative of the painting having been removed from its former stretcher and frame in the course of plunder.

There were several sets of tack holes in the canvas showing its previous mounting, but it showed no evidence of having been cut from its previous stretcher. This, as one writer observed, suggested that there had been time to make a careful removal. Following this observation was a speculation as to whether the painting had been rolled, as it might be for transport, but there was no cracking of paint consistent with a direction of a roll.

Remarkably for a picture of its age, the canvas had not been relined. It carried the grime marks one would expect from both its stretchers, but was otherwise wholly without markings or labels. While not proof, it suggested that the picture had remained in the same ownership for a long period of time – centuries – and had either been handed down, or privately sold.

This could explain why it had not appeared in any sale catalogues or in the *catalogue raisonné.*

The work done in Buenos Aires had been thorough. The pigment, ground and other chemistry was good, and style comparisons comprehensive. Whether any subsequent tests had been done, I didn't know.

I finished reading the *dossier* shortly after midnight, and reviewed the conclusions again in the morning before going to eight o'clock Mass.

I couldn't fault the picture or the report. The evidence was indisputable; the speculation on the *provenance* sound, and the logic incorporating the scientific data with the presumed historical chronology tight. It all left little doubt that this was an unknown Jan Steen.

Nevertheless, something niggled. While I had told Hawsley that I believed in innocence until proof of guilt, I had to admit that in spite of the evidence, I was uneasy. Perhaps it was because these two unknown pictures had surfaced which was deemed so improbable as to be impossible.

Before all the scientific tests were invented, the art world relied on expertise, experience and *connoisseurship*. However, the money then involved was a fraction of today's demented markets, in consequence, absolute authenticity wasn't as critical. Until the late nineteenth century, "Attributed to" was as good as "by." Even "studio of" made little difference: the painting had quality, had been done by or supervised by a master, and, like a piece of furniture, if it came from Thomas Chippendale's workshop, it was a Chippendale. (I knew a painter who, as a teenager, hung around Rodin's *atelier* where his father was an assistant. According to him, "Rodin never put chisel to marble in his life.")

Whether the auction houses wished to fudge the attribution of this painting by calling it "studio of" Steen or some lesser attribution would, in my view, be pusillanimous. However, I had no doubt that the publicity generated by the sensational discovery of a visually old and masterful painting would close the price gap between the lesser attribution and the absolute statement that it was by Steen.

Am I getting too cynical in my old age?

When I got back from Farm Street, I wasn't certain that Sophie still wanted to see me for breakfast. I knocked on the door of her set shortly before nine expecting to be greeted by a dishevelled and dischuffed Sophie, but she was obviously expecting me and looked her usual composed self as she handed me a mug of coffee within seconds of my arrival.

"I always know when you're going to call my bluff," she said, cheerfully. "I don't know how much sleep you got, but I spent an hour and a half repacking and then rehearsed my lines until nearly two. At least I'm not driving today."

Sophie seldom drove, and the same was true for me. Everything we did was in the centre of things, and having a car in central London was no asset. When we went to Paris, the Metro and taxis were sufficient and, if we went anywhere else, it was easy enough to hire a car.

Sophie seldom let me nearer her kitchen than the doorway, so it was there I stood while she prepared omelettes and bacon, and warmed the croissants. Like mine, her repertoire was limited but always well prepared. When we cooked for ourselves or each other, we didn't starve.

You hear about actors moving to a different plane when they prepare for a role. Some become distracted by the character or their situations and analyse the parts for days.

Sophie approached her acting with a pragmatic attitude. She would talk about the story, working out how and why things happened as they did.

"If the script is well-written, the motivation of the character is already there," she said. "Between the playwright and the director, there are enough interpretations of motivation. It doesn't need me to get in the way.

"Looking for 'something new' in a play or a part is usually a sign of insecurity – or just that the director has no idea what to do."

Only relatively recently has the American-style temperament come into British theatre, Sophie once told me.

"It receives very little tolerance. They don't understand that most British actors don't consider themselves celebrities."

Over the years, I had visited Sophie backstage after performances and, occasionally, at a rehearsal. When not actively busy, she – and most of the other actors – would chat to the stage crew and technicians. They knew most of them by name from previous productions over the years and would ask about their families, holidays and children's exam results.

This relationship was foreign to American prima donnas – female and male. Treat stagehands badly and the doorknob comes off when you go to make your grand exit.

Content with her upcoming role, our conversation at breakfast was relaxed and informal, ranging across topics, until she came to the matter of what I was doing for Brooke & Sons.

"You're dying of curiosity, aren't you?" I asked.

She giggled.

"I can only tell you what I told you last night," I said, and repeated that I had been asked to review evidence to support a picture's authenticity.

Of course, she was dying to know the artist, but I told her that would have to wait.

"Since when is painting authentication your expertise?" she asked, more in curiosity than a challenge.

I decided to give her the answer that she was known to give me:

"You don't know *everything* about me."

ରେ

I had only one live sitting during the week, and several portraits to finish. There was another that had been brought in for varnishing. With Sophie out of town, I could give full attention to clearing my studio during the day and focussing on the two rogue paintings in the evenings.

I cooked for myself for most of the week, but went to the club for lunch on Wednesday and dinner Friday.

There was a congenial drones table at lunchtime and a group of regulars rotated through between noon and three. Conversation was nearly always good, but if not, the food was.

There were some interesting people that day, and they included me in their conversation. There was little I could contribute to container handling logistics, but it was diverting and, occasionally, amusing.

Saying I'm a portrait painter is often a conversation-killer. "Painted anyone famous?" is the predictable comment. I'm often tempted to reply, "They are now," but modesty forbids.

Enjoyable though the company was, none of them showed any signs of going back to work, and I was anxious to read about the Rembrandt.

It was nearly three-thirty when I finally settled down at the dining table with the stack of papers on the version of *The Storm on the Sea of Galilee*. The folder contained a number of detailed photographs of it as well as side-by-side comparative images of the whole thing and details.

Both paintings were the same large (160 x 128cm) size, but the known one was portrait format and the recently discovered one landscape.

Dealing with such a familiar image, it was very difficult to be objective, so I made a few notes of my initial impressions and then continued looking. The photograph of the back of the "new" picture was interesting as it had inventory stickers dating back to the 1930s. The first was just a series of numbers on a label that said Invicta Pictures. It was followed by inventory numbers for several other defunct production studios until it reached the more modern ones: American International Pictures, Filmways. Later online research showed that Filmways had been sold to Orion Pictures and then MGM and Amazon.

The *provenance* recorded nothing more than the story of the widow trying to sell it. The name of her husband was there, but I could find no evidence that anyone had bothered to check the Internet Movie Database to see what films he'd worked on.

Sloppy.

I would do this myself later.

There was a note that no one knew where any of the papers from Invicta Pictures were, or even if they still existed. This was not surprising as I had found that most of the people at my bank thought that "archived" meant "shredded." As a result, huge swaths of information were lost on a scale greater than during the world wars. Every time a company was taken over, the cataloguing systems were different, and, as most of the legacy company's staff had been fired, no one knew where a damn thing was. More recently, this was complicated by incompatible computer systems and legacy software as each company was taken over.

Invicta had been taken over so many times that the current owners were probably paying rent on a warehouse full of stuff that they didn't know existed. I chuckled thinking that this painting might have only narrowly escaped the fate of "Rosebud" at Xanadu.

I cursed the differences in the presentation of the Steen and Rembrandt reports. The fact that one was in metric and the other imperial didn't help.

After about an hour, I was able to make sense of the paint analysis, and I couldn't see anything amiss. Like the Steen, the canvas had never been relined which suggested that it had spent most of its life in temperate conditions. The California heat can't have been good for it, but it still appeared to be sound.

One of the last photographs showed it in its frame. I went through the documents to see if there was a mention of the frame, but there was not. To my eye, it looked like a modern frame, probably put on the painting in the 1930s to match the décor of the film set.

Finding any films it was used in might yield something. I would try to persuade Hawsley that it was worth pursuing.

There was a reasonable analysis of the brushwork, but if I were handling the painting, I'd want it done again. The same would be true if I were buying it. There weren't enough examples, and many of them were comparing it to the known version of the picture that no one had seen in thirty years. Scientific photography and imaging had come a long way since then.

By Friday, I had finished the evaluations and made a few notes. I took them to the club in the evening where I expected to find Hawsley, but there was no sign of him.

I joined other friends, two historians and one anthropologist, for dinner and we had a diverting evening, free from any talk of art. I listened, quite willingly, to a discussion about the importance of the new moon in Babylonian astrology which turned into a spirited debate that extended from the dining table to the bar.

Listening to learned men discuss their interests is a pleasure too seldom enjoyed these days, and it awoke a childlike sense of wonder in me of the extraordinary diversity of people, their interests, and things that mattered millennia ago.

On my return to my set, I was both excited and enervated. Keeping up with the conversation had not been easy, but I was filled with a sense of innocent discovery, and knew that the next day, I would have to do something different to my usual Scholarly Saturday.

Chapter V

On Saturday morning, I paid the bills, said no to the invitations and decided that Hawsley's absence the night before was fortuitous in that it gave me time to do some empirical research.

Packing my notebook in my coat pocket with my headband magnifiers, I walked to the National Gallery.

The collection has ten Jan Steens and one "After Jan Steen" of which six were currently on display, most of these are in Rooms 26 and 27. I found them easily, and I scrutinised them and compared them to the photographs of the recently discovered painting. I put on my magnifiers and moved closer as the visitors moved on.

For what I do, I don't need great strength, so the magnification is only 5x – also, they are cheaper than you think. Mine don't have any illumination, which would have had museum guards panicking. As it was, I only looked odd, and I can live with that.

Many museums now have microwave sensors that sound an alarm when people get too close to paintings; never mind that visitors might have spent a lot of money for a ticket and the picture they are charging to see has minute details.

Everything I saw of the Steen paintings in the National Gallery was consistent with what I had seen in the South American one. Oddly, in some ways, the "new" one was better than those in front of me, but I couldn't yet articulate why.

When I had finished looking at the Steens, I went to see some Rembrandts.

The National Gallery has eighteen paintings by Rembrandt along with a number of those identified as "Probably by Rembrandt," "Follower of Rembrandt," "Pupil of Rembrandt," and "Imitator of Rembrandt." Of the "certain" Rembrandts, thirteen are on display; twelve in Room 22. *Belshazzar's Feast* is in Room 24.

It was this latter painting I thought I'd begin with since it was the only one on a similar scale to *The Storm on the Sea of Galilee*. I reasoned that Rembrandt's technique would be influenced by the scale, and therefore, be closer to this one than to the more personal portraits. Also, the degree to which he used assistants and apprentices might be determined.

Belshazzar's Feast was painted c. 1636 and the known *Storm* c. 1633. (For brevity, the Isabella Stuart Gardner's *Storm* will be referred to as *Storm 1* and the Hollywood picture as *Storm 2*.)

I had enlargements of both pictures with me as I stared at *Belshazzar's Feast*. As I moved from a photograph to the painting, raising and lowering my magnifiers, a school group came by and listened with admirable attention to the guide. I stood back out of the way, but a girl of about fourteen kept glancing back at me. Unfortunately, there is no way of letting people know in such situations that one is not going to do something shocking.

The guide finished, and the children dispersed to look at other paintings in the room. Surprisingly, the girl came up to me.

"Are you going to steal it?"

I took off my head magnifiers.

"It's rather big, don't you think?" I asked. "I'm not sure I could move it on my own. Perhaps you could help."

She regarded me with tolerance.

"You're doing something important," she said, confidently.

"I am."

I showed her the two photographs.

"I know *Belshazzar's Feast* is by Rembrandt, and this one," I indicated *Storm 1*. "But this one, I'm not sure about."

I let her hold the photos. She looked back and forth at them and at the painting on the wall.

"Would you like to try these?" I offered the magnifiers.

She was wary for about half a second and put them on. She had to hold them on because they were far too big for her. Once she focused, she stepped towards the painting and her mouth opened.

"There are so many small brush strokes!" she said. "How long does that take?"

"Probably not as long as you think," I said. "Rembrandt would have had people helping him, mixing paint, cleaning brushes, painting the bits without much detail."

She pulled off the magnifiers.

"That's *cheating*!" she exclaimed, loudly enough to attract the attention of her teacher, who watched us carefully.

"Not really. An architect, or even a builder doesn't do all the work himself," I said, but she didn't look convinced. "Now, before your teacher comes to take you away, which of these do you like best?"

She looked at both photographs, thoughtfully.

Before she could speak, there was a disturbance in the gallery. Girlish squeals and shuffling feet. The teacher stopped stalking me to look around. The girl with me didn't look up.

"This one," she said, definitely, pointing to *Storm 2*.

"Why is that?"

"Two things: the swells are better and the boat and the people look as though they are in more danger. *And*, it's a seascape, isn't it?" I nodded. "Well, landscapes and seascapes should be – bigger!" she exclaimed, spreading her arms.

The cause of the disturbance now approached me.

"Are you going to introduce me to your friend," Sophie asked.

My young companion was visibly shocked to see Ligeia Gordon standing in front of her. For a moment, she just stood there, eyes wide and mouth open, but then looked back and forth at us and, inevitably, asked me:

"Are you her father?"

Sophie side-stepped the question adroitly.

"Would you like me to sign your leaflet?" Sophie asked her.

"Yes, please!" she nodded.

"What's your name?"

"Jessica."

By the time she'd finished her message, Jessica's teacher arrived, but now she was apologising, rather than telling off, as had been her original intention.

"I'm so sorry she interrupted you," the teacher said. "Jessica, go join the others."

"Jessica was charming," I said, when she had gone. "It was Miss Gordon who interrupted *us*."

The teacher had now recovered her authority.

"Just as well," she said, curtly.

When we finished laughing, I looked at Sophie.

"You're back early and, you've been following me!"

"Guilty, she laughed. "I was on the other side of Haymarket and saw you. It was naughty. I'm sorry."

"No you're not," I chided, gently. "You were being nosey."

The trouble with being friends with actors is that you can never know if they are sincere. I had known Sophie for more than a decade and hoped I knew her well enough to trust her (though the matter of the murder continued to lurk in the shadows).

"Well, it's a good thing I was," she retorted. "I can't have you get arrested for picking up underage girls in the National Gallery!"

I wasn't going to win this, so I gave up.

"We can go to the National Café and I'll tell you what I've been up to."

She glanced at the retreating gaggle.

"Can't we go somewhere else?" she asked, glancing over her shoulder, as people continued to whisper and point.

I agreed. We wouldn't have a private conversation here. Having been recognised, there would be no escaping attention.

"I didn't expect you back until tomorrow," I said. "Did they sack you?"

"The shooting went well and my part had been shot," she explained. "Someone was heading to Skipton late yesterday afternoon and gave me a lift. When I got back to Albany, you weren't around. I was tired and slept late before going down to Her Majesty's Theatre to reserve some tickets for friends on the crew. I had just come out when I saw you and followed you."

As we walked up Haymarket, Sophie put her arm through mine. Given her token display of displeasure in the gallery, this surprised me.

We walked in silence, then, as we neared Piccadilly Circus, she spoke.

"You know, Jessica is about the same age I was when we met," she said, seriously.

"Yes, but I'm not," I said. "By the time she's as old as you were when we met again, I'll be dead."

Sophie didn't reply, but by the time we passed St James Piccadilly, she was holding my hand.

෨

When we were settled in a quiet corner of the bar, I told Sophie that a painting had recently come up that could be another version of a Rembrandt. I didn't make it sound remarkable or mysterious, but she guessed that Hawsley had asked me for my opinion.

She accepted this at face value and was more interested in the painting than where the picture had come from. I had said Los Angeles, and that was a likely place for a Rembrandt to be.

She remembered the Gardner heist but not any details of the picture until I showed her. When she had seen both of them, I asked which she thought was better. Like Jessica, she chose the landscape version.

I told Sophie the title of the painting, which I had not done with Jessica. Even so, the knowledge that Christ was in the boat – and that His image was larger in *Storm 1* – didn't affect her judgement.

"It's a more frightening storm," she said. "The cropping – well, the composition – of the portrait version looks contrived by comparison."

And so, it was. I hadn't appreciated that, but that's why these things take time. Could it have been that *Storm 1* was a trial version for *Storm 2*?

Probably not. Both were finished paintings, and looked like they had been finished by the same hand.

I raised the question with Sophie.

Her laughter filled the bar.

"Poor Nigel, you always make things so complicated," she said. "These are religious paintings."

"Yes, so?"

"So, someone came into the studio while old Rembrandt was working on the portrait version and said, 'What a great image for my church! There's a chapel where it would be perfect. Can you paint me a vertical version? – It could have been the other way round, of course."

Occam's Razor strikes again. *Why not* two versions for two different churches? Artists frequently did two versions of the same subject. Sometimes more.

I – and probably Hawsley – had been focussed on the provenance and authenticity.

Could *Storm 2* had been painted before the famous one? Perhaps there would be a clue in the X-ray or infrared images. Not being expert in reading them, I had done little more than to see if there were evidence of either being a palimpsest.

Another thought came to me.

"How are your contacts in the film world?" I asked Sophie.

"Ah!" she exclaimed, catching on to my train of thought. "You want to find the film that the painting appeared in."

"It's not necessary, but it could provide a date reference to work from, and I'd like to add something to the information Hawsley gave me."

Sophie laughed.

"That's called pride or vanity, and you'll have to confess it," she teased.

"It will be lost in the list," I replied. "Anyway, I think this is more in the category of professional help to a friend. Possibly worth time off in Purgatory."

She giggled again. Her lack of understanding of my faith could be amusing. So far, I had resisted telling her about the Sacred Monkeys in the Vatican.

"You can add self-delusion to the list," she retorted.

I gave her my bored look.

"Can we get back to the point," I said. "We should be able to create a list of the films the owner worked on, even if we have to start with the total output of Invicta films. It was only in business for a few years from 1933 to 1940."

"What did the owner do?"

"I'm not sure. The name of his widow is in the papers. His might be too," I said. "We should be able to trace him."

"Could I try doing that?" Sophie asked. "I'm better on the computer than you are, and you can do the fusty stuff that you do."

Chapter VI

After returning from the club, I went into my study and began finalising my comments for Hawsley on the Steen and Rembrandt.

To me, there were two fishy things: first, that these unknown paintings had surfaced within a few months of each other, and, secondly, that both were by Old Masters. Had they been by third or fourth-string painters, they would still have grabbed headlines around the world and excited prices.

The question was: did this indicate anything about their veracity? Did being from the premier league – which would ensure very close scrutiny – increase the probability of them being real? Or was it a double bluff?

I wrote all this down even though all I needed to tell Hawsley was that I found nothing amiss in the scientific findings. I also recorded my comments about the excellent job done by Gwilym Jones & Stottlemeyer compared to that of Weisman & Rossi.

I included my feeling that the "discovered" *Storm 2* was better than *Storm 1*, and probably pre-dated it. That would really set the cat among the pigeons, but it made sense and was what I had come to believe.

All I wanted to do now was add some stills from the films *Storm 2* appeared in, which would prove that it wasn't a post-war fake, opening another line of inquiry.

Aware that I might be duplicating some of what Sophie was doing, I began some preliminary research.

The painting had come into the possession of Karl Beckman, whose widow was the picture's current owner. Beckman, I learned, was a German who had moved to the United States in 1935 during the rise of Hitler, having seen the writing on the wall. He had worked for Sofar-Film Produktion until 1932 when he moved to Studio Babelsberg. Soon after, he moved to Hollywood. No doubt he had colleagues who had moved there earlier who eased his entry.

Invicta Pictures had been set up as what today would be called a joint venture company to enable several small studios to work together to produce an epic film to rival those of Paramount and other large studios. It was producing a Civil War picture modelled on *The Oresteia*. While it did reasonably well critically, it was upstaged by Eugene O'Neill's *Mourning Becomes Electra*, and barely made its money back. This limited its output to one or two pictures a year, until it was bought up and merged into the studios featured on the inventory labels on the stretcher.

Like many industry pioneers, Beckman could do every job on the lot, but he was mainly known for lighting and cinematography. It was in the latter capacity that he worked for the successor studios.

I assembled a list of films he had worked on that I was certain was incomplete, but decided to let Sophie pursue the rest and see if she could turn up copies of some of them.

Beckman's widow, Carole (after Carole Lombard?), had married him around 1960 when he would have been over fifty and she half his age. Now, some forty years after Beckman's death, and in her eighties, she had decided to offload the painting.

That was the simplest narrative, and there was no evidence for it.

I had painted – and listened to – enough writers and professors to recognise that this was the basic difference between American and British scholarship. The American "thesis" approach would posit a theory and look for evidence to support it. The British would look to see what was there and then construct a narrative.

A firm believer in the British approach, I had read enough philosophy to know that asking, "What if?" enough times could evolve a narrative when little evidence was available. It was like dead (deduced) reckoning that could provide a workable hypothesis when there was only the old datum.

We had only the pictures and had to trace backwards to see where they came from.

I finished my notes for Hawsley on Saturday night and re-read them Sunday afternoon. My final line gave me more unease than anything else I'd written.

"While I can find nothing wrong with the findings for either picture I am left with the uneasy sense that something is wrong."

I wrote a further paragraph and crossed it out. I had two more attempts at articulating my reservations and crossed them out, too.

Hawsley had asked me to evaluate the findings, not to venture an opinion. Nevertheless, I felt a moral duty to note my misgivings.

In the end, I added the phrase, "though seeing the actual paintings may dispel that feeling," which partially assuaged my conscience.

I had finished other necessary business and had just settled into my armchair with a glass of Gamay and the latest copy of *Apollo* when the telephone rang. I suspected it was Sophie as very few people knew my Albany number.

"Nigel. John Hawsley."

We exchanged pleasantries before he moved to business.

"How are you getting on with the research review?" he asked.

"I finished this afternoon," I said, relieved that I had.

"Excellent. Can you do lunch tomorrow?"

"The club is shut for lunch Mondays," I said, "but we could go to The Green Room."

"Perfect. One o'clock."

The Green Room was the restaurant in the Keeper's House. While at the Royal Academy, it was a place frequented by Friends of the RA rather than people from the art world. They tended to use their own clubs or The Arts Club in Dover Street.

The risk of what we would discuss would be less likely to be overheard, or if it were, it would not be fully understood.

და

Sophie stopped by Sunday evening to say that she was travelling again. She was going to Manchester for rehearsals for a revival of *The Philadelphia Story* at the Corn Exchange.

"That's a bit dated," I said. "Won't people watch Katharine Hepburn, Cary Grant and Jimmy Stewart for half the price?"

It's a four-week run and it's nearly sold out," she said, smugly.

"Oh. Is there someone good in it?"

"You do like to live dangerously," she replied. "It's still fun, but the trouble with it is that people will keep expecting us to start singing."

"Who's playing Tracy Lord?"

"You don't know how hurtful that is," Sophie teased. "I always wanted to play that part."

She named a well-known young lady of "A-List" celebrity status.

"Can she act?" I asked.

"No one will care, they just want to see her breathe," she laughed.

"And you're – "

"Margaret Lord. Her mother," she said, resigned to her age.

"I am sure you will be suitably condescending. I'll try to come up to see it."

"Book soon," she said, and gave me an air kiss. "Keep out of trouble."

❧

I resisted the temptation of looking, yet again, at my report for Hawsley and slipped the two files into a carrier bag and went to meet him.

He arrived shortly after I did and we chatted as we looked at the menu and ordered.

As I was still considering going to my studio after lunch, I drank only water. Hawsley confined himself to a single glass of Sauvignon Blanc.

"I won't keep you in suspense, John," I began. "Bottom line: the process for both paintings is sound, though the presentation a bit ragged on the Rembrandt. I can see nothing wrong with the interpretation of the data."

He nodded and looked encouraged.

Our meals came and we stopped talking shop, resuming over coffee.

I took him through my thought process, but he was more interested in the bottom-line, so I told him that I thought both pictures appeared to be real.

"I'll tell you one thing, though, John," I said, trying to sound authoritative, "if the Gardner *The Storm on the Sea of Galilee* ever surfaces again, I'd take a long, hard look at it."

Hawsley looked concerned.

"Do you think it's one of Berenson's optimistic attributions?" he asked.

"Not at all," I said, easily, "Berenson was the best of his day – and he had a very long day. He made mistakes – we all do – but no one has ever seriously maintained that any of them were ingenuous."

There was a famous case in the 1920s about a disputed version of Da Vinci's *Portrait of an Unknown Woman* (then called *La Belle Ferronnière* – a work discussed in my previous book). Three experts had examined the painting in Paris and reached a unanimous decision that it was not by Da Vinci. Roger Fry, Sir Charles Holmes and Berenson made up the panel. The storm had blown up because Joseph Duveen had publicly refuted the authenticity of the painting without having seen it. However, when a court case was opened against Duveen in New York, it emerged that Berenson had worked for Duveen. Everyone's reputation took a knock, and, in the absence of a consensus of the jury, the case was settled out of court. The authenticity of the painting remains in doubt. In 2010, it was sold by Sotheby's in New York for $1.5 million.

"Berenson's reputation isn't what it was," Hawsley observed.

"You can't libel the dead, so people will say anything to get attention, especially in the frenzied art world," I continued. "However, I think we do have to entertain the real possibility that the Gardner *Storm* was painted *after* the Hollywood one. I continued. "The composition of the landscape version is better, and everything else I can see indicates that it's the real thing."

"It would be great to be able to *prove* the new one was the earlier work," Hawsley replied.

"Would it add value if it could be proved?"

For a second, Hawsley hesitated, unsure if I was teasing him.

"Probably, but not much," he said. "It's rare enough for a Rembrandt to come on the market but one this size and of a familiar image would attract a lot of interest."

For interest, read money.

I paused. Hawsley knew something else was coming and waited patiently.

"I know you didn't ask for a comment on their authenticity, but I'm giving you one anyway."

He nodded, cautiously.

"My report," I began, pointing to the carrier bag, "includes this opinion: Even though all the scientific data looks good – and this is hard to describe – there's something that doesn't ring true."

Chapter VII

Hawsley did not look surprised. He said nothing, but drank some coffee and leaned back in his chair. A waiter appeared, but instead of asking for the bill, Hawsley asked for more coffee. He didn't speak again until after it was poured.

"It's fitting that we just mentioned Berenson," he began.

He said it in a tone that gave nothing away, but only suggested story-telling.

"The days of Berenson, Duveen, and the others have given way to the forensic scientists. These new miracle workers have uncovered some of the errors made by men who had nothing to rely on except their eyes, intelligence, experience, and maybe a sixth sense," Hawsley said.

"The other day, someone made a similar observation about doctors," he went on. "You go to see your GP and tell him you have backache. He asks where and you tell him, and he consults his computer. Indeed, he looks at the computer more than he does at you. He prints out a prescription or suggests you go for physio, and only when you turn to go, does he see the knife in your back."

I gave a cautious grin, not certain where this was headed.

"Do we trust the observation and examination of the doctor more than we trust the computer – and *should* we?" he asked. "I think – and if you quote me, I'll deny it – that we should start training experts in observation again; that we are relying too much on forensics. Heresy, I know."

He drank his coffee then leaned forward.

"I'm not a natural at this. I was born into Brooke and had to be trained to live up to its expectations," he said. "I know my field of operation, and it's the commercial side, but I can see our 'experts' becoming more reticent to make judgements, and they rely more on the scientific examinations.

"And, here's the thing: I trust your judgement because I have known you for twenty years. I believe you *know art*. I feel entitled to be sceptical of the scientists because I don't know them or their machinery from Adam," he said. "Their work is amazing: x-ray and infrared images of things that haven't been seen in hundreds – even thousands – of years are not to be brushed aside, but we must not surrender our human judgement.

"What gives me some sleepless nights is the number of pieces that we sell that may not be genuine. It's a percentage that's unacceptable, but no auction house or dealer can afford to have every work forensically checked."

He waved his hand.

"I know, it's no excuse, and the public doesn't want too many old men around, and the young ones have insufficient training and experience. Time was when people who had been around art could recognise lead paint by a combination of its colour and condition, now they do a biopsy with thousands of pounds of equipment – but your instinct – *and mine* – say it's wrong."

He paused and leaned back.

"The market can accept two Old Masters being discovered – but we can't explain why these haven't been noticed before – especially the one in Los Angeles," Hawsley said.

I gave a laugh, and he regarded me with suspicion.

"Sophie gave me a hard time about something similar this week," I said. "She accused me of over-thinking the two versions of the *Sea of Galilee*."

Hawsley looked up with curiosity.

I told him her scenario of someone coming into Rembrandt's studio and ordering another version but in a different orientation.

"It's the same with it not being recognised in Los Angeles," I said.

He didn't appear to have caught on.

"If you went to the home of a film technician and saw a large Rembrandt, or Reynolds, or even Jasper Johns on the wall, would you – for a minute – believe it was real? Of course not.

"There are still lots of undiscovered paintings around. Most of them are probably in plain sight. Large numbers of paintings have been left – with no identification and little or no provenance – to institutions where there is no particular expertise.

"Small American colleges received tons of effects from gilded age millionaires and it's taken decades to catalogue it. Much has only received a cursory look. One small women's college discovered that the rather nice picture of the Virgin that had been hanging in its chapel for eighty years was a Veronese," I said. "The art world may be relatively small, but the 'art net' has a very coarse mesh, and a lot slips through."

Hawsley considered this, and sighed.

"There are so many variables," he said, wearily. "Look, there's nothing for it," he continued. "Can you come to Amsterdam with me to have a look at the Rembrandt?"

"What could I contribute that your people couldn't?" I said, trying to hide my excitement at the prospect.

"I don't pay you," he replied. "Besides, you're on the other side of the art world and, frankly, you have no reputation to be damaged."

I laughed, rather loudly.

"It sounds like fun," I said.

"*It's not fun!*" he snapped. "*It's the credibility of the market! Fortunes could be lost!*"

I'd finally hit the nerve.

"I don't give a damn about that, Jack," I said, calmly, knowing the effect of his informal Christian name would have.

For a moment, I thought he was going to throw the wine bottle at me. He glared at me, red-faced, then burst out laughing.

"Has anyone told you that you were a bastard? You're right, damn it," he conceded. "And, I suppose, you'll have to do, unless you know anyone else who could be more objective than you."

I thought.

"If you're serious, I just might."

ঔ

It was now late enough that it wouldn't be worth going to the studio, so I returned to Albany. On the short walk home, I remembered Sophie's parting words and hoped I would stay out of trouble.

The prospect of going to Amsterdam and being one of the first people to see a newly discovered Rembrandt was exciting.

As Hawsley had said, I was on the other side of the art world. Selling direct or through the Royal Society of Portrait Painters or the Royal Academy, I never had to work with dealers. Prices were agreed before the start of a picture, and I had a long relationship with good framers who worked with me or with my clients. Dealing with an artist whose portraits were invariably a metre square was good business for them.

It worked smoothly and simply, and I could stay on the periphery of the more colourful but less respectable part of the business. Back in the days of John Singer Sargent, art dealers, like his good friend Asher Wertheimer, were regarded as only marginally better than money-lenders. Today, the dealers and auction houses had a well-tended façade of respectability, but it didn't do to look too closely.

By asking me to view the Rembrandt with him, Hawsley was not only taking a risk, but enabling me to be privy to a realm that was Byzantine in its protocols and approaching cabalistic in its language.

Though I had never said it directly to anyone but Sophie and a few other close friends, the attitude of the dealers was essentially that a picture was worth what someone was willing to pay for it. The business of connoisseurship, if truth be told, was eighty per cent bluff.

During my undistinguished days in the Royal Navy, among the hundreds of books I'd read was John Fowles' beguiling indictment of modern art, *The Ebony Tower*. In it, the reclusive old painter, Henry Breasley, builds up to a devastating assault on contemporary art by lambasting the "connasewers" and "Pickarsehole."

Similarly, there's a delightful exchange in Alan Bennett's *A Question of Attribution* between the Queen and her Keeper of the Pictures, Sir Anthony Blunt. Blunt is examining a painting whose attribution is being debated. The Queen asks him if he sees it as part of his job to prove that her pictures are fake.

While humorous, the exchange raises questions about the importance of the exact identification of authorship, for it is something that affects only the value of the painting and not the painting itself.

Is there not something wrong with an appreciation of art that is influenced by who painted it?

There is also the problem of prejudicial context to overcome. The fact that a painting is hanging in a museum loads the dice against objectivity.

Undergraduate psychologists love playing with these notions.

There's a simple, popular experiment:

"I'm going to show you photographs of two paintings. This is a picture called *Wheatfield with Crows* by Van Gogh. What do you think of it? Use of colour? Composition? Impact?"

The replies are noted.

"Now, I am going to show you the last painting Van Gogh created before he went mad."

The same photograph is shown.

"Of course! Look at the blacks – and those threatening skies." "The crows are like angels of death (or Dementors in today's vernacular). The yellow is a sure sign he's rolling off his trolley."

The fact that no one knows if *Wheatfield with Crows* actually was Van Gogh's last painting, or whether he was actually mad, isn't relevant. The point is that people's *perception* has been enhanced – or corrupted.

People see what they expect to see. The moment a picture is pronounced a fake, it looks completely different. "That colour is wrong," "This hand is clumsy," "That shadow is coming from the wrong direction."

Is this because people are essentially uncomfortable with art? Ill at ease in museums? In automatic awe of the great names?

I wish I knew.

༄

Returning to Hawsley's comment, I did know of someone who might be more objective, if he could be tempted out of retirement.

My old Cambridge friend, Bill Warren was a retired Detective Chief Inspector. While he had no interest in art, I knew that, from time to time, he had worked with Scotland Yard's Art and Antiquities Unit. It was Bill who had told me that less than fifteen per cent of stolen art was ever recovered and other interesting titbits.

It was also Bill who had introduced me to James Beech after he had made the headlines solving a theft and forgery case about twenty-five years ago. He was only a decade younger than Bill and me. He would probably be retired, but he might be bored, so it was worth a call to Bill.

James Beech was a curious chap. He had gone straight from a comprehensive in Leeds into the Police Academy. The first part of his career was honourable but undistinguished. He did nothing wrong, but he was what you might call a plodding plod.

When Dick Ellis was setting up the Art and Antiquities Unit in 1989, he was looking for people who knew about art. However, he also needed muscle and people for the normal drudgery, and Beech volunteered. He knew little about art, but more than anyone suspected.

As the press reported – and Bill supplemented – one day, the team was sitting in the Tate or the National Gallery with a handful of recovered paintings that needed to be confirmed as fakes. Beech was there along with one of Ellis' deputies. The room was full of experts who looked at the paintings, the backs, labels, varnish, *craquelure* and other normal giveaways. It is serious work, and they proceeded carefully before concurring that they were all clever fakes.

Everyone was about to go when Beech spoke up. Until then, he had only done paperwork and carried equipment and pictures.

"Would it be possible to have another look at that one?" he asked very politely, and the experts were so taken aback by flunky flatfoot that they picked up their magnifying glasses and huddled over the picture again.

After a few minutes, the experts looked up and asked what, if anything had prompted him to ask the question.

"I could be wrong, gentlemen, but it struck me that the canvas might be on the wrong side of the stretcher."

This is not an unknown occurrence when artists stretched their own canvases. There is usually a slight chamfer, or bevel, on one side of the wood so the canvas doesn't deform on the inner edge of the stretcher or pick up resins from the wood.

One of the curators tapped the canvas an inch or so from the edge of the picture – which was still in its frame – and nodded.

They fetched pliers and a screwdriver and removed the picture from the frame and examined the edge. They discovered two tacks holding the canvas were missing, and there was one tack that was modern.

Bill told me that it became comic for a while, as each of the experts wanted to take the painting back to his own gallery or laboratory for examination. In the end, the inspector said the work was again "of interest" to the unit and that one of its members would supervise all further examinations.

The re-examination went on for days. Beech scrutin-ised the process and his brain sucked up every bit of information about the language and procedure that it could.

The upshot was that they found that the forgery had been painted on top of a valuable stolen painting, a variation on an old forger's trick.

Usually, a forger would find an inexpensive painting from the right period and paint the more valuable forgery on top of the old canvas.

Beech had detected the reverse: a valueless image on top of a valuable one, ensuring that it could be moved, undetected, anywhere in the world. As would be expected, Beech's instinct for fraudulent art became legendary at the yard.

However, it did have its downside. On more than one occasion, a much treasured painting, stolen from a stately home or museum, when recovered was pronounced a fake by Beech. Forensic investigations ensued and, too often, Beech was proved right. The involvement of the insurers in what could have been a conspiracy to commit fraud meant that Beech's presence wasn't always welcome.

For these reasons, I hoped he would join us.

74

Chapter VIII

I called Bill on Sunday evening and outlined the situation and how I thought this could suit Beech extremely well. Bill wasn't certain that he would be tempted as he was enjoying his retirement so much. After twenty-five years of dealing with pompous owners, curators and experts, Bill said Beech's view of the art world was pretty jaundiced. Nevertheless, he said he'd pass on my message.

Inevitably, Bill and his wife, Virginia, wanted to know about Sophie. They had met at Sophie's cousin's funeral, and Virginia had kept in touch with her.

"When she gets back from Manchester, ask her to give Virginia a call," Bill said. "I think she wants to go shopping."

We chatted more about some old friends, but he didn't mention art again except to ask me if I was still busy.

"It seems like the lockdowns incubated a good deal of vanity," I said. "I have one or two requests every week. It would have been wonderful at thirty-five, but not now. Besides, I think a good number of them just want a painting by me so that when I pop my clogs the value will shoot up. They think they don't have long to wait."

"Now there's an idea if you ever write another one of your intrigues," Bill laughed. "Commission a series of paintings from young artists and murder them to capitalise on the sensation."

"I'm glad you said 'young artists'," I said, amused by the idea.

"Yes," he laughed, adding, "Make them all arrogant abstractionists. Throw in some slashing of paintings, threats that close galleries and clever sabotaging of competitions and awards ceremonies."

He was getting uncomfortably close to the upheaval that could be caused by too many unknown masterpieces.

"Why the vehemence against abstracts?"

Bill snorted.

"There seem to be only two good reasons for abstract art," he said, in an ambiguous tone: I couldn't tell if he was joking or not. "First, because no one can tell us our opinion is wrong, and secondly, because it sells."

I laughed.

"There are more reasons than that," I joined in. "Don't forget that it's a failsafe way of attracting attention for no good reason and with minimal effort."

Bill laughed. Views like his kept me self-critical. While I had a solid reputation and some respect among other artists, I don't have the public reputation of a creator of controversy.

Bill concluded by saying he'd contact Beech and try to tempt him. Hopefully, what he relayed would be just intriguing enough to pique his interest.

ᚲ

On Monday, my life returned to normal. I arrived at my studio in Southwark shortly after nine and prepared for the ten o'clock sitting.

My concession to "retirement" was that I now only had two portraits underway at a time, and this gave me time for visiting galleries and museums, having leisurely lunches and dinners with friends, and attending concerts and lectures.

Already, the rich programme of free concerts and lectures was returning. Having been unable to perform for nearly two years, musicians were eager to put themselves in front of an audience. Churches that had lost much of their already meagre income were ready to open their doors for anyone who might attract a crowd.

Sophie had introduced me to the secrets of cheap matinee tickets for many shows (out of the tourist season), and events at the National Galleries, National Film Theatre and cinema clubs. The Royal Academy and the Royal Society of Portrait Painters had programmes that I could indulge in, too.

However, even a painter can have too much art, so I began attending talks at the V&A, the Science Museum, the Royal Institution, Gresham College, the RSA and

London's other extraordinary institutions, each with a long history of public lectures by notable speakers.

After two hours painting a noted biologist who talked about anomalies in the genome of Magnapinna squid, I had to steel myself to attend a lecture on artificial intelligence – or A.I. as they insisted on calling it.

I'm afraid that made it hard for me to take the lecture seriously. The speaker said, "A.I.," so often that all I could think of was the song *Cielito Lindo*, or American cheer-leaders warming up.

However, my early career as a mathematician kicked in, and I learned quite a lot. It was certainly more interesting than squid DNA.

The week progressed in a similar vein: a delightful Renoir film, an unusually good exhibition of genre painting, and a refreshingly honest talk on the Etruscans. (The bottom line is that, despite lots of research, many theses and countless PhDs, no one knows who they were or what their works mean.)

"Like the Druids," the man next to me said as we stood to go.

"The Druids?"

"They're mentioned by Julius Caesar and twice more in ancient texts, but the rest is speculation or fabrication," he said. "For all anyone knows, the Druids were make-believe boogeymen used to frighten children into obedience. At least the Etruscans left us some stuff worth looking at."

❧

I didn't hear from Sophie until Friday afternoon. She knew I was usually back at my set after a long lunch at the club and timed her call with frightening accuracy.

For an actress, Sophie talked very little about herself. She did tell stories about fellow actors, performances, and audiences. These were anecdotes, not gossip (she was remarkable in her ability to keep confidences).

"I always forget what a lovely play it is," she said. "It's well constructed, the characters are just exaggerated enough to be amusing but remain wholly believable. It's still funny, and satisfying."

"Presumably, the audiences are sharing your opinion," I ventured.

"You know the Royal Exchange: I can be outside the auditorium and hear everything – and see a lot," she said. "Not a single line has fallen flat all week."

She then went on to tell me about the various actors, their roles and things that happened during performances. It took very little time as there was a meeting with the cast before a light meal.

"I do hope you're keeping out of trouble," she said in closing.

I thought I had been until I began reading my post. Unusually, there were two handwritten envelopes along with circulars designed to look important as well as several magazines.

I looked at the envelopes. Modern stamp cancellations reveal little of the origin of letters anymore (probably some perverse interpretation of GDPR), though a scan suggested one hand was masculine while the other feminine (if one is still allowed to say such things).

I opened the masculine envelope and found it was a short note from James Beech. It simply said that he was, indeed, intrigued by what Bill had told him and gave me a London telephone number.

Turning the other envelope to open it, I saw an embossed return address, "Bickering Place" with a post code. I withdrew the stiff card.

Dear Sir Nigel,

Sophie Gregg, an old Cambridge friend, said she knew you, so I am taking the liberty of asking if we can discuss having a portrait painted.

I appreciate that you are busy, and there is no rush to have this done.

Yours sincerely,

April Fisher Gilliat

There was a telephone number, but I wanted to talk to Sophie before dialling it.

Much safer to call Beech first.

తొ

I had met Beech once half a dozen years ago when I accidentally encountered him with Bill Warren while walking home from my studio. I bumped into them in Cockspur Street. I presumed them to be *en route* to the new New Scotland Yard, but looking back, they were more likely to have been headed to Christie's.

It was a very brief encounter with none of us saying much more than good afternoon when Bill introduced us. I remembered nothing about Beech apart from his stocky build and, in the brevity of the meeting, didn't associate him with art crime until after I'd moved on. I remember feeling that I'd missed an opportunity to say something about his work.

When he answered the phone, I could immediately visualise him again. It was a strong voice, not loud, but authoritative. I identified myself, and it softened, but remained business-like.

"I have learned of two paintings that are causing some consternation," I said, after the opening pleasantries. "These pictures – "

"Before you go any further," Beech interrupted, politely but firmly, "I infrequently act as a consultant on art fraud. I don't solve crimes or catch bad guys. I don't run tests or undertake comparative studies, and mostly I enjoy the peace and quiet of my retirement."

"Then you'll like this puzzle," I said, unfazed. "Two Old Master paintings have surfaced in different parts of the world. Both have passed the normal examinations and tests, but Sir John Hawsley has reservations, and I agree with him."

There was nearly a minute's silence.

"So, it's you two against the art world, eh?"

"Yes."

Silence.

"Tell me more," he said, and I sensed a warming of his tone.

"Until things are finally established, this has to be treated with police-standard confidentiality," I said, hoping it didn't sound too pompous or condescending.

"I think we can do better than that," he said, and I could hear amusement in his voice.

For the next twenty minutes, I gave him the bones of the story. He asked a few perceptive questions, then said what I hoped he would.

"I'm in."

Chapter IX

It was now time to find out how serious Hawsley was about having another opinion. I knew there was a risk that he had considered our exchange to be persiflage, but I also knew that he would not turn down the services of a detective inspector who had worked with the Art and Antiquities Unit.

I also knew he would pay; the reputation of Brooke & Sons demanded it.

Both presumptions proved to be the case. I think he was astonished that I knew Beech well enough to ask him, which, like much of my life, had been a combination of an ability to see through people and bluff. Hawsley even refrained from comment when I told him Beech's terms. Since he wasn't paying me (other than expenses), he'd be able to justify it as the cost for two "consultants."

"I think Beech would like to see both paintings," I said. "If they somehow have a common source, then it's only sensible if it can be arranged."

Hawsley didn't reply immediately.

"Would it be possible for the three of us to meet?" he asked.

"I think that would be possible. Beech lives in London and should be available."

"Good. Can we see if we can arrange something for early next week? Lunch or dinner at Mountfield Gardens?" he suggested.

"I think that's a good idea," I agreed.

"Out of the glare of the art world," he said. "I doubt any members would recognise him."

"Unless they've been nicked."

ℬ

On Tuesday, I sent a holding note to April Gilliat saying that I was interested in the requested portrait, but that it might be a week or two before my schedule opened up. I promised to call her, and noted that Sophie had enjoyed her time in Lincolnshire.

In the afternoon, I had a short sitting with a surprisingly charming woman who was CEO of one of the larger banks in the City. Call her Gillian. Not only was she refreshingly engaging – chatting easily about her children and what they liked her to cook for dinner – but she also walked from the bank to my studio. She left the dress, some make up and the simple jewellery she wore in the portrait in the bedroom closet and changed on arrival.

Gillian was an easy sitter, but trying to settle on the pose had taken a long time. She wanted something that the directors would like that suited the gravitas of the bank and her job, but she didn't want to look pretentious or self-important.

"I don't want to look like a frump, either," she said.

We had discussed a number of approaches and settled on a composition of her in a three-quarter pose looking out of her office window.

"The office once had a good view, but then another, taller building was built, and I look out on a glass wall," she explained. "Too often I have to have the curtains drawn so the chap opposite and I don't stare into each other's offices."

That became the portrait: a clever, but essentially ordinary lady in a cold, sterile corner office (the photos of it were grim – she said she didn't dare bring in pot plants and flowers for fear of ridicule) looking onto another, cold, sterile building.

I created the effect of looking in one window to see her looking out the other. This gave me the chance to put in some strong diagonal lines and areas of subdued grey and blue. She wore a smart suit, slightly brighter than navy, and we set it off with a vibrant Hermes scarf – the only real colour in the picture apart from her eyes and flesh tones. I knew I'd be accused of creating a Norman Blamey sort of portrait, but that would be easy to live with.

Gillian had the good manners to turn off her mobile phone and leave it in the bedroom during the sitting. It was something that I usually requested, but she did it before I asked.

Since she was only able to stay for an hour, we needed more sittings. I asked if it was an efficient use of her time, especially with the walk.

"Most of what a bank CEO does all day is unnecessary," she replied. "They usually just meddle in other people's business and make silly promises to large shareholders."

I asked if large shareholders didn't deserve to be kept sweet.

She laughed easily.

"I had the good fortune to train in Paris at Banque de Saint Lazare with Louis-Philippe Du Moncey. He took a small, staid, bank and developed it to be the third largest bank in France.

"As you know, customer service is a somewhat alien concept in France," Gillian continued. "I was in his office one day when his secretary interrupted to say that the company's second largest shareholder was on the line."

She named a prominent New York investment bank.

"Louis-Philippe took the call, listened for a while, then said, 'That's not something we'd be interested in doing.'

"Sensing an imminent row, I stood to sneak out, but he waved me back to my seat.

"He held the phone and listened for a while longer, making no expression. After a time, I gathered that the caller had stopped talking and Louis-Philippe was taking his time responding, I then heard, 'Hello? Are you still there?' as he tipped the phone towards me, before replying.

"'Dick,' he said, calmly. 'Your bank invested in us because you liked what we were doing. If you don't like what we're doing now, you are free to sell, but, please, don't tell us what to do.' And, he hung up."

She smiled.

"I learned a lot from that. If investors don't like what you're doing, you've got the wrong investors."

I stopped painting.

"That was risky. Couldn't they have voted the bank's management out?" I asked.

"That's exactly what I asked," she replied. Louis-Philippe said, 'Everything is a gamble, but it would have been far more risky – and expensive – for them to sell out than to hold their position.'

"In this case, they put up with it."

Conversations like that one have made my career fascinating, and, on the strength it, I made a small investment in her bank.

಄

A telephone call from Hawsley early Wednesday morning accelerated my week. I was preparing to walk to Southwark when he called to see if Beech and I could meet with him for lunch at the Lansdowne Club on Thursday.

I could and asked if he wanted me to contact Beech.

"I asked him first," Hawsley replied. "I thought he might be less available than you are."

I laughed.

"I know you; you're predictable. I don't know him," Hawsley added, in explanation of what he assumed I had taken as presumption. "We'll be there at one o'clock.

"If you have a sitting, I'm sure you can move it," he added.

I had no sitting but could not resist saying, "I'm sure HRH won't mind coming another day."

There was just enough of a pause to even the score.

"I'll see you then," I said, before he could reply.

The Lansdowne has been much improved since I first visited it. The renovations in the swimming pool finally cleared the persistent – and legendary – algae in one of the far corners and the addition of the awning has made outdoor dining a popular pleasure.

Beech was at reception when I arrived and told me that Hawsley had been summoned to admit us. After greeting us, he led the way to the bar and then to lunch.

Our conversation was surprisingly relaxed and grew more so when Hawsley and Beech discovered a mutual interest in fishing.

I was immediately out of my depth, but they chatted about rivers and streams they'd fished, the rods and reels they'd used, and fly-tying.

In a matter of moments, these two men, who had been strangers only minutes earlier, were sharing tips and laughing like old companions.

"I think it's clear what we must do when this is over," Beech said.

Hawsley cheerfully agreed and then asked Beech if he owned any pictures.

"Only by the forgers I nicked," he said. "They are the only ones I can afford whose authenticity I can be assured of."

It was delivered in a cheerful – almost cheeky – way, but it hit Hawsley between the eyes.

When all but our coffee cups had been cleared, Hawsley turned to business.

"Change of plans. The painting from California is coming here. It should be with us next Friday. I will accompany it to the Courtauld, and you are both welcome to attend the uncrating."

"That's a coup," I said, admiringly. "How did you manage that?"

Hawsley smiled.

"It was mostly Langton's work," he said. "He's been in touch with Weisman & Rossi from the beginning and alerted me. I think he persuaded them that dealing with the British would be easier than dealing with the Rijksmuseum at this stage."

Beech laughed.

"A totally unwarranted conclusion," he said.

"I believe Langton just asked how good their Dutch was, then asked if they might prefer having it handled via London," Hawsley laughed. "We'll have it looked at by the Courtauld. They will repeat the tests, and we'll take both sets of documentation with us to Amsterdam."

"Will we review the results before we go?" Beech asked.

"Oh, yes. The Courtauld will present its results at the end of the week. We should all be there and can discuss them then," Hawsley said.

Beech nodded.

"The timing is fine," he said.

Hawsley turned to me.

"I took on board your comment about the presentation of the report from Weisman & Rossi and had my office create a series of spreadsheet pages using the format from Gwilym Jones & Stottlemeyer. In addition to its own report, the Courtauld will fill in the spreadsheet so we can compare data sets. The Courtauld won't see the Weisman & Rossi results."

"Do you expect there to be a difference?" Beech asked.

"No. I expect the results to be essentially the same," Hawsley replied. "It should just be a question of presentation. I'm not expecting there to be anything to question."

"And that is the nub of the problem," I said.

We each appeared to consider what this meant for each of us. The best – and the worst – outcome would be for Beech to believe the pictures to be genuine. The excitement, publicity and financial gain would be spectacular, but it would be a professional indictment of Hawsley's judgement, and a personal one of mine."

"I brought a copy of each report for you," Hawsley said to Beech. "Read them and let us know what you think, and we can talk again when we have had the chance to see the painting on Friday."

As Beech and I left the building, I hoped Beech didn't regret becoming involved.

"Seeing people at the top of their game is always interesting," he said, "whether an Old Master or a forger.

"This should be a safe enough diversion," he added. "Forgers are seldom murderers, and I can work with Sir John; all the best people fish."

Chapter X

Friday was a surprisingly bright day and I could feel the early warmth of the sun as I walked to Somerset House. Hawsley was going to meet us there at ten. He had emailed to say that the painting had arrived safely and had been handed into the custody of Brooke & Sons.

James Beech was chatting with someone at reception when I arrived.

He introduced me to Guy Stone, the head porter, whom he had known for many years. One of the curators who would inspect the painting and direct the testing was on her way down.

Hawsley had given both Beech and me explicit instructions not to express any comments that could prejudice the opinions of anyone at the Courtauld. This would be difficult on seeing a large unknown Rembrandt for the first time. However, I suspected Beech was as experienced in holding his tongue as I was when confronted by a piece of hideous art painted by a friend.

Beech and Stone were talking about old friends when the curator arrived. I had met Helena Stirakis several times before over the years through both the R.A. and Royal Society of Portrait Painters. She looked and acted

93

like a socialite, and also looked much younger than I knew her to be.

She was a good art historian, but an even better curator and had assembled some excellent thematic exhibitions juxtaposing known and unknown artists from all periods to stunning effect. I admired her boldness and the sure-footed mounting of her exhibitions.

Unsurprisingly, she knew Beech, too.

After greeting us, she led us to one of the great studios on an upper floor where several paintings were on tables or easels in various stages of conservation or examination. None of them looked particularly interesting.

"Guy will supervise the removal from the crate and then accompany the painting up here with Sir John," she explained. "We'll have a look at it on the easel and then examine it, front and back, on the table."

"Will we be able to see it out of its frame?" Beech asked.

Dr Stirakis had to consider this, which surprised me.

"That should be possible," she conceded, but she gave the impression that it was an inconvenience.

Her mobile phone rang, and she walked away from us to take the call.

"You know Dr Stirakis?" Beech asked me, quietly.

"Only from social events and exhibitions. You?"

"I fear I exposed several pieces in the collection as either misattributed or fakes," he said, *sotto voce*.

"I bet she's just delighted to see you, then," I said.

"The picture is on the way up," Dr Stirakis said, walking back to us. "Have you read the Weisman & Rossi report?"

We said we had, though Beech and I had not had the chance to compare notes on it yet.

"I haven't seen it," she said. "Sir John wanted to ensure objectivity."

Neither of us commented, and we waited in silence for the lift to arrive bearing the painting. Beech withdrew a pocket police-style notebook from his jacket and made some notes.

The freight elevator arrived, and Hawsley stepped out, greeting us as though it were Christmas.

"This is quite exciting," he exclaimed, unashamedly. "I am as eager to see this as are you all."

Supervised by Guy Stone, two men wheeled a trolley to the table, removed heavy quilted packing blankets, and a lighter blanket. They lifted it onto the table, cut the strapping and began unscrewing the lid.

It would be a while yet as there was another blanket and then a envelope of bubble wrap about three layers thick. The picture had to be removed from the crate before this was cut open and the painting extracted. All we could see was the back.

Almost without pause, the men lifted the picture, checked its orientation and placed it on the large extruded aluminium easel and secured it in place. Guy Stone went to the opposite wall and switched on the lights.

Although the room was suffused in daylight, the focused artificial lamps made the picture dazzle, and we moved forward, gaping in silent wonder.

It was a stunning piece – whoever painted it.

Hawsley could not refrain from an expletive, and Dr Stirakis also expressed admiration of the picture's impact.

"It's disconcerting to see such a famous image – but not quite," she said.

I had, in the mid-1980s, visited Boston to speak at MIT and Boston College and visited the Isabella Stuart Gardner Museum and seen the known version. I had noted it as a rare Rembrandt seascape and had only paid more attention to it than to many of the other paintings because of my time at sea with the Royal Navy. At that time, I had no inkling that art would become my long-term career.

One by one, we approached the painting and using various torches and magnifiers, examined the image. We let Hawsley go first, followed by Dr Stirakis. I was next and put on the headset that had amused Jessica in the National Gallery, and Beech went last.

It didn't take long for me to confirm the impression made by the photos in the report. Beech took slightly longer, but not as long as I thought he'd take.

When we'd finished, the painting was placed face down on the table on a soft clean blanket, and we moved around examining the back, the stretcher, the stretcher bar, the condition of the canvas and the labels.

"These labels are a history of Hollywood from the 1930s," Beech observed, pointing to the various names.

Dr Stirakis produced a soft but stiff brush and brushed a small section of the canvas, raising dust from the fibres.

"I expect it had a light hoovering in Los Angeles," Hawsley said, "if only to make studying it less of a dirty business."

We looked for a few more minutes.

"Can we remove it from the frame?" Beech asked.

I glanced at Dr Stirakis who looked about to object, but Hawsley spoke first.

"That shouldn't be a problem," he said, easily. "They installed these bracket hinges in California rather than drive nails back through the stretcher."

We leaned forwards to see the nail holes. There seemed to be three along the top and bottom and two on each side.

Dr Stirakis motioned to Guy Stone who produced a screwdriver and swivelled the clips out of the way. The men then gently grasped the stretcher and lifted the picture from the frame.

"Front or back?" Stone asked.

Hawsley glanced at Beech.

"Image side up," he said.

This gave everyone a chance to look at the painting close up again. Beech inspected the edge of the canvas and the tacks. He took out his notebook again and made an additional entry.

The unframed painting was returned to the easel and the frame was placed on the table. It was judged to date from the early 19th century, but nothing else useful was found.

"Does anyone want to see anything else?" Dr Stirakis asked.

No one did.

"Then, we'll move this upstairs and begin work."

The men secured it back in its frame, wrapped and put it on the trolley.

"Will you join us for lunch, Sir John?" Beech asked.

"Thank you, no," he replied. "I'll follow this upstairs, and then I need to get back to Dover Street. I'll keep you both in the loop on the progress of the tests.

Beech and I left the building, walked down the Strand but said nothing about the painting.

"Simpson's all right for lunch?"

80

Throughout lunch, we talked about everything except art and the painting. Beech told me more about the various forms of flies, casting, rods, reels and assorted paraphernalia. As I would have expected, he was very traditional and used only the necessary equipment and no flash wind-up, battery or digital gadgets.

He spoke with a knowledge and enthusiasm that made it fascinating, far more interesting than many of my more distinguished sitters.

By the time the coffee arrived, he was telling me how individual species could be caught, and I realised he was no longer talking about fish.

"And how has our forger made his fatal error?" I asked.

He smiled, pleased to have been understood.

For a plain-speaking man, he had much subtlety. I supposed that's what enabled him to understand both the criminal forgers as well as the collectors.

"You agree it is a fake?" he asked.

"Yes."

"Why?"

"I don't know," I admitted, spreading my hands. "The documentation is sound; the tests are conclusive, but something is not right."

Beech nodded.

"I agree with everything you say," he said.

"You know Sir John doesn't believe it's real, either?" I asked.

"I inferred that from the way he spoke to me. His problem is that the experts will want to have a hand in 'discovering' it, and all the test results will support them."

We were silent for a moment, then simultaneously spoke:

"But, by God, it's a wonderful picture!" we exclaimed.

We laughed so loudly that a few remaining diners turned towards us.

"Have you no idea what's twitching your whiskers?" Beech asked.

I was well-aware of the seeming stupidity of what I was going to say. I took a breath.

"It's too good."

Beech looked up, sharply.

"Explain."

I told him how I had gone to see the Rembrandts in the National Gallery and had spent a long time looking at *Belshazzar's Feast*.

"They were painted within about five years of each other," I said. "I am assuming that both versions of the *Storm* were painted about the same time – if it's real."

"Yes," Beech agreed. "If we are wrong, and the painting is genuine, then, they were probably in the studio at a similar time."

I told him Sophie's theory.

"I'll buy that," Beech said, "but I still don't think it's real. Tell me why you think it's 'too good'."

I was on very thin ice now, for his ordinary copper demeanour, his experience and expertise in this area were indisputable, and far greater than mine.

"Looking at the different areas of *Belshazzar's Feast*, it is possible to detect areas that were painted by assistants or apprentices. They are faultless in form, colour, tone, texture and so on, but the brush work is different. I can show you if you want. Each artist has his own favourite type of brushes, and while many will have been shared, anyone good enough in the final stages of a painting will want to use his own.

"Here is the artistry: he will create an identical effect of the master, but the structure – the direction and pressure – of the stroke will be slightly different. It can be like recognising when a writer sharpened his quill. The handwriting is the same, but the marks are different."

"Fingerprints, I call them," Beech said.

"Fingerprints," I repeated, musing. "Yes, that's just right."

"All right, that's *Belshazzar*. What about this landscape *Storm*?"

I thought a moment.

"In your language, there's only one set of fingerprints, and it's unlikely that an artist at that stage of his career will have done the whole painting from start to finish."

"But an apprentice might have," Beech suggested.

I froze. That option hadn't occurred to me.

"Think about it," Beech said. "Just as Ligeia Gordon suggested, someone came in to see Rembrandt, saw the portrait version of the Storm in progress and orders a landscape version. Rembrandt is happy to accept the commission, but has a new project, and delegated what is essentially a copy job to an apprentice.

"Oh, Rembrandt would probably have laid out the composition and maybe even drew some pencil sketches of the slightly different orientation of the boat. He may have also changed the scale of the wave formation to suit the landscape format."

"In those days, it was the subject that was important, not who painted it," I said. "If it came from Rembrandt's studio, it was a Rembrandt.

"It's rather the way we regard those we call 'designers' today," I continued. "We don't expect that Yves Saint Laurent *made* every shirt and tie that we wear, nor do we expect that he even designed everything that has his name on it, fabric or garment. But, it was made in his *atelier*, and met his standards. So if a painting was a Veronese or a Montemezzano didn't make a damn bit of difference."

I was very satisfied with this scenario, and so was Beech.

"Exactly. If this was the case, we've also established which version was painted first."

I beckoned for more coffee and was about to enjoy a drink of it when Beech shocked me again.

"That's all well and good," he said, "but I don't think it was done by an apprentice. I think it's a twenty-first century fake."

I put my cup down.

"Why?"

"I have no idea," he said. "I guess we'll just have to find out."

Chapter XI

On my way back to Albany, I stopped at the National Gallery to have another look at *Belshazzar's Feast* to ensure that I hadn't exaggerated what I had said to Beech. When I had done that, I visited Room 29 that houses 17th century French paintings.

Never a fan of that period, I thought I should give it another chance, or re-enforce the reasons for my dislike.

The religious and secular paintings suffered from the sort of fantasy world imaginings that populate contemporary video games and *bandes dessinées* and have no basis in the reality of the Old or New Testament worlds. To me, they present a barrier to understanding the messages of either.

Also disappointing is the imposing portrait of Cardinal Richelieu. I am always sorry not to like this as Champaigne's triple portrait of him hanging next to it is a favourite of mine.

Why disappointing? Basically, because it's bland and not very good.

This is hardly surprising as the portrait has been copied so often – including multiple times by Champaigne's own workshop – that the repetitions and variations have worn thin like too often copied versions of film transparencies. Even though the National Gallery's version might be the original Champaigne, there are better versions all over the world. In all of them, however, the head looks disproportionately small, which surely was not the case in real life. The face is dignified, but expressionless. There is no warmth, no sense of humanity. There's not even pride or haughtiness.

While Richelieu was an imposing figure and a major force of his time – giving good reason why artists should be careful when portraying him – he was far from Dumas' villain.

In this version, the pose is awkward with his eminence holding his *biretta* away from his body for no apparent reason. Is he playing with an invisible child or dog? Perhaps he's gesturing to an invisible taxi or omnibus.

His face doesn't give us any clues, either. In other versions, the *biretta* is closer to his body, but it still looks clumsy.

In the better versions, he holds a letter in his left hand. Here, he rather coyly lifts his cape to show the lace edge of his alb. Given the pink satin rather than the eponymous red, the whole lower half of the painting gives the impression of a courtesan. Starting at the feet and moving upwards, one might expect to encounter the bust and face of a notorious harlot, rather than the era's leading diplomatist and prince of the Church.

Even the background is bland. It is indicative of neither temporal nor heavenly power. It's the sort of backdrop that was used by 19th century photographers. All that's missing is a potted palm.

The figure does not sit (stand) well in this portrait. His proportions are out of kilter with the background, and the shapes of the drapes and archway have no harmonious echoes in those of Richelieu's robes, or positions of his arms and hands.

The more one looks at it, the more it looks like the figure was cut out from a child's book and stuck into place on one of a number of possible backgrounds.

A platform at Saint Pancras might have been a more sympathetic setting. Francis Bacon might have done something interesting, perhaps replacing the hat with a Beretta.

ᘓ

I left Trafalgar Square feeling that I had sat through a bad movie and at the same time thinking I had missed something.

I once attended a lecture at the R.A. that I considered one of the best they'd ever hosted. The speaker had made an excellent case for not spending time with art you didn't like. He maintained that if you could articulate why you didn't like it, and believe that those reasons were not blind prejudice, then your judgement was probably sound.

He went on to list paintings and artists he didn't like. This produced amusement as well as consternation. A good discussion began, but the speaker made the fatal mistake of suggesting that affected admiration for art one didn't actually like was a continuing manifestation of "Puritan guilt."

Had he said, "Catholic guilt," there would have been no problem, as only eight percent of the population would have been offended, and far fewer in that audience. He was questioned about this more than anything else he'd said. He gave reasoned answers that upset enough people that he was never invited again. Fortunately, I have been able to hear him elsewhere.

For those who might be curious, he said after the Tudors had destroyed more than ninety percent of British art, there was little for the Puritans to do apart from removing the remaining colour. They had set themselves up as the arbiters of taste when they had none, and their lasting effect could be seen in the dull colours worn by any crowd of British people today.

Realising that he was in blood stepped in so far, he continued to suggest that racial prejudice stemmed as much from the colours worn by Indian, African and Caribbean immigrants than that of their skin.

While the academicians didn't resort to violence, the noise was considerable.

Private discussions continued for some weeks, and included the affrontery of the Pre-Raphaelites to bring colour back to English art.

Of course, what really stung was the chap was essentially right.

∞

I had just opened the door to my chambers when the telephone rang.

I glanced at my watch. It would be Sophie.

"Hello, darling!" she said in her round, warm voice that barely concealed laughter. "Have you been good?"

"I have more commissions than ever," I said. "And you? How are the performances?"

"Still good, on the whole," she replied. "Bad weather last night thinned the house, but it made up for it in enthusiasm and laughter. Only a week left."

"I look forward to seeing you," I said.

"You say that because you can't avoid it," she laughed. "How's your little job for Sir John?"

"I saw the Rembrandt today."

"And?"

"It's very big."

"But is it by Rembrandt?" she pressed.

"The Courtauld is making tests this week," I replied.

"Yes, *but what do you think?*" she asked, with rising frustration.

"I had a note from April Fisher. She wants me to go to Lincolnshire and paint a portrait."

That stopped her.

The silence was longer than I expected.

"What did you tell her?" she asked, her voice very subdued.

"I wrote back saying I'd have to look at my schedule to see when I could get away from London."

"Tell her never."

"You're going to have to tell me why," I said, amused that I had predicted Sophie's reaction correctly.

"It's not a good idea," she said.

"Why? Won't she pay me?"

"Oh, she'll pay."

I had the sense Sophie wasn't talking about money.

"Do you think she won't like the painting?" I asked, innocently.

Sophie was quiet.

"She'll like it," she said, sounding defeated. "I expect you'll get on very well. She always liked older men."

I laughed.

"Is this jealousy I'm hearing?" I teased.

"You know it's not."

"Then what?"

"Possessiveness."

Navigating my relationship (a wholly inadequate word to describe human interactions) with Sophie was a matter of the tides, shifting sands, the seasons and the phases of the moon. There was care, affection and a sense of normality for Sophie; for me, it was undemanding companionship. It was a modern tragedy that one of the most attractive personalities and top actresses could not bear to be touched.

In spite of this physical detachment, there was a good deal more emotional dependency than either of us wanted to admit. Hence, there were sudden, unexpected outbursts of jealousy that Sophie would only call "possessiveness."

After her expression of displeasure at the prospect of painting April Fisher Gilliat (and going to Lincolnshire to do so), we spoke of other things, though I told her very little about the Hawsley project.

Just before we finished the call, Sophie said:

"I think you could do a wonderful picture of April at her home. Just don't let her talk you into staying at Bickering Place."

Chapter XII

I wrote to April Sunday evening and suggested she telephone me at her convenience to discuss the portrait and the arrangements. I posted it Monday on the way to my studio.

My week progressed on its normal routine. I painted an opera singer and a university chancellor, and finished the portraits of a high court judge and Gillian, the banker.

I had scheduled a "Varnishing Day" for each of them. I didn't varnish, but it was the sitter's final chance to make changes.

I would put the portrait in a frame on the easel and unveil it to give it a sense of occasion and freshness. This was usually followed by champagne.

Some sitters would just look, say, "Fine," and be on their way, wondering why I had made them come in. Others would engage in the fun.

It was not unusual for subjects to bring spouses, children, business colleagues or friends. It was also not unusual to go to lunch or the pub afterwards.

On the rare occasion that the reception was not favourable, I'd have them look at the picture in the mirror to see it as they saw themselves, but since they had all seen the picture throughout the sittings, people were seldom surprised.

M'lud, the judge, felt compelled to do a summing up for an invisible jury. This lasted nearly ten minutes, during which his lordship demonstrated a spectacular ignorance of composition, colour, tone, technique, art history and taste. His stentorian delivery was a *tour de force* of erudite vocabulary, misapplied rhetoric and mangled syntax.

When he finished, he looked at me expecting a rebuttal, but I just gave him his coat.

By contrast, Gillian loved her portrait and gazed at it in silence for five minutes. From what I could tell, she spent very little time looking at herself.

"This is amazing," she said, when she turned to me. "It's bold, but also very subtle."

She turned back to it as I opened the champagne.

"It's too good for a bank boardroom," she said, turning back to me and taking her glass. "Do you suppose it would be possible to exhibit it somewhere, first?"

This delighted me. I was able to submit a number of pictures to the Royal Academy Summer Exhibition and had only one candidate so far, and there were other possibilities.

"I think that can be arranged," I said.

She chatted easily, eventually suggesting we go to lunch.

She gave very little of herself away, but spoke mostly about a charity she was chairman of.

"Of course, they just want the name of the bank, and were quite taken aback when I told them I wanted to go to the Gambia and work on a project with them for six weeks."

She told me that what this group was doing was focused, efficient and delivered visible results quickly.

"Its projects are relatively low-cost and can be replicated around the country and yield some real results."

All of this resonated with my education, and I envied her the chance to go.

"Aren't you afraid of a boardroom coup in your absence?"

She merely shrugged.

෬

On Wednesday, there was a concert at Festival Hall featuring a young Russian pianist who played the Bortkiewicz Second Piano Concerto, for the left hand (no, I'd never heard of it either). It was one of the ones written for Paul Wittgenstein. I found it a brilliant and exciting piece that, had it been written forty years earlier, would have been in its *melieu*, but then it wouldn't need to have been for the left hand.

On Thursday (this chronology is mostly to enable me to explain myself to Sophie on her return), I had a telephone call shortly before leaving my studio. I thought it would be from Hawsley with details of our proposed meeting the next day at the Courtauld to hear the test results, so I was surprised to hear a woman's voice.

"Sir Nigel? This is April Gilliat. Do you have time to talk?"

ଞଠ

I decided to forego the club and returned to Albany. With my post, there was a note from Hawsley saying that Dr Stirakis wanted to review the test results over the weekend and that our meeting would be at ten o'clock on Monday.

This suited me as I wanted to tidy my studio and buy more supplies. It was always enjoyable to walk through London to visit the art supply stores and see what new things they might have.

I always shopped for my own materials, but had my metre square canvases delivered. Cheap imports had led to a fall in cost but also in the selection. There was little choice in canvas weight, stretcher quality (polythene keys forsooth!), and they invariably used staples instead of tacks. Steel staples tend to be too thin and prone to rust – especially here with the high humidity.

As I have noted elsewhere, I have, on occasion, stretched my own canvases, but you need to do a good number to make it cost-effective, and then you're faced with storing the materials and tools, as well as the work of sizing the raw canvas with hide (or rabbit skin) glue, and, if being pedantic, mixing your own gesso with more hide glue and marble powder. I did this while at a painting workshop not long after it became apparent that painting would be my career, and while fun, it becomes little more than an affectation, like those who grind their own pigments.

So, my shopping trip included a litre of turpentine, cobalt dryer, and a handful of colours. I also collected a loaf of French bread and a clump of spring onions as I fancied egg drop soup for a modest Friday meal. It is a favourite of mine, and over the years I'd perfected three versions that suit my moods. Since Sophie would be back Sunday, I did not expect her to call, but the telephone rang about twenty minutes after my return.

"Last performances!" she said, excitedly. "It's gone very well and everyone is keen to finish on a high. Wednesday had a few rough spots but it came back together quickly."

She continued to revise her lines to be word perfect on the final nights.

"I can't wait to get home and be sloppy," she said, actually sounding tired.

"You're not sloppy."

"I only let you see what I want you to see."

"– said the actress to the bishop."

She ignored this.

"I can't have the chambermaid going around saying that Ligeia Gordon lives like a pig. Each afternoon, when I leave for the theatre, the room looks ready for a new occupant. One has to work at a reputation," she said.

She asked about the mystery painting, and I told her about the day.

"Will it ever go on public show?"

"I expect a museum will buy it," I said. "The Rijksmuseum is the obvious one."

"What else have you been up to?"

I took a deep breath.

"April called. She sends her love and hopes the play is going well. . . ."

"You're stalling," she scolded. "What is it?"

"April doesn't want me to paint her. She wants me to paint her daughter."

"Marissa?"

"She's only got one. She wants me to go up the week after next and stay until it's finished," I said.

"Why Marissa?"

"I don't know. Thirty-eighth birthday present?"

"Don't be facetious," Sophie scolded. "She wants a full metre square?"

"Yes. Has she ever seen yours?" I asked.

"She's seen pictures of it, but I don't think she's ever seen it. She's never been to Albany. What do you think her game is?"

"You think it's a game?"

"Did you tell her what the painting would cost?"

"Yes."

"And hotel and food?"

"Yes."

"And car hire?"

"Yes."

"And she *still* wants you up there for a week? That's a lot of money," Sophie said, no longer amused, but concerned.

"Darling!" she said, suddenly. "I've got to go. I'll see you Sunday. Cook me something nice."

଼

I was able to have an uninterrupted Scholarly Saturday, reading and listening to music before going to Farm Street. This was followed by dinner at the club. Nothing I did that day had anything to do with art, and my mind felt fresh when I returned, and I rewarded myself with a bedtime murder mystery.

Apart from their entertainment value, murder mysteries are rich social documents of their time. They record décor, manners, attitudes, prejudices, fads and itemise the objects found in homes and used in daily life. Often, these possible clues stimulate ideas of what to place in portraits.

As one who reads for pleasure, I never actively try to "solve" the case, but it often becomes evident, no matter how many red herrings are dragged across the trail.

৪১

It was dark enough at about six on Sunday to see a light on in Sophie's set across Rope Walk. She'd come over around seven. After the run of the play, she would either be exhausted and only fit for macaroni cheese, or she'd be high on adrenalin and would chatter until one in the morning and then collapse.

I could only guess which it would be, but would know as soon as she walked through the door.

I was roasting potatoes and vegetables and would cook a pork sirloin (betting on the adrenalin high) when she arrived. I opened a bottle of *Cuvée de Vatican* that she had given me a few weeks earlier.

At two minutes past seven, there was a quick knock on the door, and she let herself in.

"Gin! I need gin!"

I had guessed correctly.

I greeted her and received two air kisses and a brief hug.

The fixings for the G&Ts were already prepared, so she was able to take her first mouthful within two minutes of her arrival.

"Cheers, darling," she said, and sat in her usual place on the sofa, as far from me in my armchair as she could get.

She took a mouthful and smiled with satisfaction. She may have purred.

"That's the first drink I've had since leaving London," she said. "No doubt, it will go straight to my head."

"You've been on the wagon?" I exclaimed.

"You know I never drink during the run of a play," she said.

"I know no such thing!" I retorted, never having heard such rubbish from her before. "When you did that David Hare play last year, I poured drinks for you every night!"

"That's when I'm working in London," she replied. "When I perform north of Watford, I never touch a drop."

I glared at her.

"Oh, all right," she gave in. "It's only because the drink available at the parties and dinners was terrible. Cheap gin, not enough ice, flat tonic, small glasses, no lemon, and supermarket wine. It was easier and more polite to be abstemious."

"If the world only knew how you suffered."

Over dinner, I told her about my plans to go to Lincolnshire. She seemed to regard the trip with a combination of humour and caution.

"Why did you refer to April's daughter as 'slightly scary'?" I asked.

Sophie's eyes widened and she gave a broad smile.

"You *do* listen!" she exclaimed.

"Of course, I do!" I said, definitely. "When did I ever *not* listen to you?"

"I don't know," she shrugged. "Sometimes I think I prattle about nothing and you tune out. I think I would."

I said nothing for a moment, and she looked puzzled.

"Can you *please* answer the question!"

Despite being tired, she caught on, and I laughed.

"Okay. Touché," she said. "I thought Marissa was a bit scary because she seldom did or said anything expected," Sophie began. "She looks conventional – wears smart clothes for work and stylish, if clichéd, country styles at home or when she goes out.

"I never saw or heard anything about a boyfriend – or significant other – and, she's never been married. She still lives at home, but her relationship with April is rather detached. She – "

"Detached?"

"There's little obvious affection, but she's not formal or rude," she explained. "April says she'd becoming obsessed with the idea of excavating the ruin – which I never saw.

"During a walk around the garden, April told me about the house – you'll see all the clues when you get there – and she said that sometimes it was like Marissa saw what used to be there and not what actually was.

"I'm probably being hard on both of them," she concluded. "April's just lost her husband and Marissa her father.

My assessment of Sophie's fatigue was frighteningly accurate. She chatted happily through dinner, enjoyed the wine, but declined dessert. She moved back to the sofa after we'd cleared the table. I stayed in the kitchen to make coffee, and when I returned, she was curled up on the sofa, fast asleep.

I laid a blanket over her and returned to finish in the kitchen. When everything was put away, I turned out the lights and went to bed with *Death and Double Death*.

Chapter XIII

When I got up Monday morning, Sophie had left. The blanket was folded neatly on the sofa. This didn't happen often (what would the neighbours say?), and she was disproportionately embarrassed when it did.

I didn't expect to see her in the morning. I'd be leaving for the Courtauld at nine. If something didn't distract me, I'd have time for a cup of coffee.

The morning bustle was well underway when I walked along Piccadilly. Sometimes, I'd cut down the back streets to avoid the congestion, but that morning, I welcomed it like a good stretch after a deep sleep.

I expected to write off much of the day. Hawsley and Beech would probably want to talk after receiving test results. That could drift into lunch and the afternoon. Ordinarily it wouldn't matter, but I had much to arrange before my trip to Lincolnshire.

Apart from packing the materials I'd need and my lightweight easel, I'd need to hire a car and book a hotel – and remember to make the online payment for the Dartford Crossing.

On-site painting isn't something I've done too often. My studio is convenient enough so that people don't object to coming to it. However, there have been trips to

Oxford, Cambridge, some cathedral cities, a few CEO's offices, and the odd visit to Lancaster House or Kensington Palace.

The military hierarchy that I painted usually welcomed a trip to London, but wanted to be painted in their surroundings. I solved this by visiting them for the first sitting. I made some sketches and took pictures. After that, they could come to London all they liked.

I was thinking of what needed to be done before heading to Lincolnshire and was walking on auto-pilot down Duncannon Street, along the side of St Martin's in the Fields when I heard Beech call my name. His policeman's authoritative voice was instantly recognisable. He was only a few steps behind me and quickly caught up.

"We've got time for a coffee, haven't we?" he asked.

We went into whatever the Charing Cross Hotel was currently calling itself and went upstairs. It had been chopped and changed by each owner, but most who knew it still called it the Eleanor Bar, though there was presently a distinct coffee room.

"What do you think we can expect today?" Beech asked, when we'd ordered.

"I'd be surprised if the results were significantly different from those from California," I said.

"I'd like to think we did things better here," Beech replied. "The three of us know it's a fake. I'd be surprised if Dr Stirakis didn't believe that in her gut, too."

"Probably," I agreed. "But, she's not in this to tell us her gut feelings. She's there to run the tests and crunch the numbers."

Our coffee came and we returned to drink our coffee and consider our positions.

"If the Courtauld says it's genuine, it's unlikely that the Rijksmuseum would disagree," I resumed. "Hawsley will broker an amazing sale, the art world will be agog again, and another fake gets hung in a prominent museum."

"And each step adds to its pedigree," Beech agreed. "Even if the ultimate judgement was 'Studio of Rembrandt' it wouldn't knock more than a fiver off the price."

I chuckled.

"When Hawsley first told me about this painting, I asked him if it were painted over the stolen one," I said. "I'll be rather disappointed if Helena didn't discover that."

Beech looked horrified, then burst out laughing.

"Well, that would at least prove that we are right about the visible image being a forgery."

⍵

We arrived at the Courtauld shortly before Hawsley.

"This should be interesting," he said. "I've not been given a heads up one way or the other, so I'll be hearing the findings for the first time, too."

I accepted this, but sensed that Beech wasn't fully convinced. I wondered if I should defer to his great experience of liars, though I had never found Hawsley to be one.

Dr Stirakis appeared on the dot of ten and led us upstairs. This was a different studio and was blacked out apart from a light focused on the painting.

It had been tested, but not cleaned. Permission would be needed from the owner for that, and Hawsley wanted the Rijksmuseum to see it first, and preferably buy it and clean it on their guilder.

Dr Stirakis began her interminable PowerPoint presentation (why can't people just talk anymore?). We went through the methodology, a list of who carried out the work and their qualifications, and the known history of the painting.

Next came an explanation of how a small area, about an inch square, had been cleaned and the varnish tested. Paint samples had been taken from there and from along the edges covered by the frame.

"We were able to collect colours that we think represent the complete palette," she said. "These were compared to those known to be used by Rembrandt."

Dr Stirakis went on to compare the present picture with the stolen *The Storm on the Sea of Galilee*, most of which Beech and I had already discussed.

Next were the X-ray, infra-red and ultra-violet images. These were new versions of the images taken in California, and from what I could tell, they were no different with the same *pentimenti* revealed.

We, then, moved to the chemistry. While I understood it, I was only interested in the conclusions, which were unsurprising.

The conclusion was characteristically defensive: no reason had been found to question that this had been painted by Rembrandt.

Hawsley looked delighted as we were each given a copy of the thick, full-colour report that included all the slides we had just seen.

The lights were raised and Hawsley thanked Dr Stirakis for her work.

She replied with comments about how exciting it was to work on the picture, and that the team looked forward to watching its future unfold.

Hawsley turned to Beech and me.

"Any questions, gentlemen?"

I let Beech go first since he was being paid.

"The painting has never been relined?" he asked.

"No," Dr Stirakis replied. "It's in remarkably good condition. We looked at the dust and found pollen, and looked at some linen fibres.

"The fibres are long, which is characteristic of the slower-growing flax of the time, and it makes a strong canvas," she explained.

"And no signs of canvas repairs or retouching?" Beech asked.

"It's unusual, but not unheard of," she replied.

Beech looked at me.

"This is fascinating," I began. "There are a lot of labels on the stretcher, aren't there?"

"There are thirteen and signs of two more that fell off or were removed," Dr Stirakis answered, patiently. "Most, as I said, were from film companies from the time it appears to have been used as set decoration."

I paused before asking my next question.

"While the painting's life before the twentieth century may have comprised hanging on the same wall for two hundred fifty years, it somehow travelled to North America, spent about a hundred years in the California heat and was moved about fifteen times – just to put on the labels – and remains in pristine condition.

"It makes me wonder if museums aren't wasting a lot of money on heat and humidity control," I said.

Dr Stirakis waited before speaking.

"Is that a question?"

"My question is, Helena, do you not find it curious that given its rather off-hand treatment, that this three hundred eighty-seven year old stretcher, canvas and painting have suffered no damage whatsoever?"

Dr Stirakis stood perfectly still for nearly a minute before speaking.

"We have reported what we found, not on what we did not find."

I waited for her to continue, but she did not. Hawsley looked like he was still considering the probability of an unscathed picture from the seventeenth century.

Beech then asked the question I knew he'd been waiting to:

"Does this look like it was painted by a single hand?"

Dr Stirakis seemed to sense that she was being led into a trap, and she saw no way out.

"Yes, it does appear to have been," she said.

"And at the time it was painted, was that the way Rembrandt worked?" Beech asked.

He was not aggressive and sounded completely reasonable.

She stiffened even more.

Beech gave a surprisingly engaging laugh.

"This isn't a cross-examination," he said, easily. "I'm just curious."

Helena Stirakis appeared to relax a little.

"I suppose what I'm asking is, do you know another Rembrandt of this size and period that was painted entirely by Rembrandt?"

After a brief pause, she replied, "No, I don't."

"Which all goes to show what an extraordinary picture this is," Hawsley exclaimed, trying to put some noughts back on the potential value.

He looked at his watch.

"Thank you so much for your report, Dr Stirakis," he said. "It is exhaustive and perfectly clear."

We said goodbye, and while perfectly polite, Dr Stirakis treated Beech and me warily.

On the pavement, Hawsley stopped and faced us.

"We've got two series of tests and a pretty definitive attribution," he said, obviously pleased with the outcome. "The forensic data were conclusive and the signature was judged to be real. It will be for the Rijksmuseum to prove it otherwise."

There was no point in challenging him. It didn't matter what he thought personally, he and Brooke & Sons were covered.

I needed to get to my studio, but also needed to talk to Beech and to eat.

Chapter XIV

We wandered down the Strand and went into Champagne Charlie's under Charing Cross Station. Once again, we said nothing until we were seated and had drinks in our hands.

"I think Sir John was getting nervous," Beech said. "He closed that down pretty quickly."

"In fairness, he'd got what he wanted," I said.

"It's curious, though, isn't it? There's a perfectly beautiful painting, but somehow it's important whether the artist who signed might not have actually painted it," Beech mused, then added, "but, of course, we all know that that painting is less than five years old."

This was the second time Beech had called the picture a twenty-first century hoax and not one from the twentieth.

"What makes you think it's that new?" I asked.

Beech was silent.

"I'm going to sit on that one for a while," he said. "I trust you, but I'm not sure I trust myself on this yet. There are a few ideas knocking around, and all of them tell me that the painting has to be pretty new.

"I want to read the report carefully," he continued. "There may be things in it that weren't in the presentation."

"I thought that, too," I said. "I expect what we read will have even more caveats than we heard this morning."

Our lunches came and we ate.

"I rather liked Helena's line about reporting only what was there, not what wasn't," I said. "I think there might be a clue there."

Beech smiled.

"I thought exactly the same thing," he agreed. "But, tell me, as a painter, what do you think?"

I put my fork down and leaned back.

"I think there is too much money in the art world, and that has corrupted not only the market, but compromised the integrity of just about anyone dealing in it.

"It's becoming too hard to actually *see* what's in front of us. We're blinded by names and values," I went on. "For example, I don't know anyone who doesn't look at van Meegeren's Vermeers today without saying that it's hard to believe that they were anything but fakes. They don't realise that they have been *trained* to see them as fakes. The top experts in the world were fooled then, and they can be fooled today."

"I agree," Beech said. "And, that's why they lean so heavily on the scientific data – which is nothing to do with the actual quality of the art, but only with it's authenticity."

This was familiar territory. It was the Stradivarius syndrome.

In numerous blind tests, the sound of more modern instruments had been preferred over that of Stradivari. While the price of the newer instruments had shot up, the prices of the Stradivari had not been affected.

What we needed to do was prove our feelings about the Rembrandt, and there was no conventional way of doing so.

"I'm going to have to read and think," Beech said. "The usual clues aren't there. We may have raised some interesting points today, but not enough to create real doubt."

I knew I was on the edge of my competence. My major contribution had been to put Beech in contact with Hawsley. As to what I thought, it simply didn't matter. It had been an amusing diversion for me, but it was time to move on. I had Lincolnshire to think about.

On Monday afternoon, I booked the hotel and a car. I had all my materials and only had to pack a suitcase for a week.

א

Sophie knocked on my door at around eight. She had had an easy day, called her agent and gone to the gym to work out the kinks from sleeping on my sofa.

"I do have some news for you," she said, in her usual teasing manner. "I heard from Marcus at the National Film Theatre, and he's traced prints of three of the films that your technician worked on at Invicta."

I was excited by the possibility that could prove that the Rembrandt was older than Beech thought.

"He's sent for digital versions of them, and I'll watch them next week while you're being beguiled by Marissa," she said, sounding very pleased with herself.

Sophie would enjoy doing that. She knew what to look for and would enjoy watching old films more than I would. As things stood, she knew very little of the actual situation, Beech's involvement, or our doubts. This would give her some objectivity if she needed it.

"I can arrange to have prints made of the images with the painting," she said. "You can put them in the *dossier*," she continued, mocking the importance of my adventure.

"Don't make fun of my projects," I said. "You're the one who disappeared for two weeks."

She laughed.

"You'll forget all about Rembrandt as soon as you meet Marissa Gilliat," she said.

"That sounds like a warning."

"You should consider it one," she said, darkly.

I asked her to clarify her remark, but she would say no more.

෮

In my preparations to leave London, I threw the two reports on the Rembrandt into my suitcase. I'd have time to review them in the long evenings at the hotel. I also put in a few journals and a novel.

I had no intention of working more than four hours per day. Two in the morning and two in the early afternoon. I wanted to visit Lincoln and some of the pubs along the way. It would be good to get away from London and my claustrophobic world.

I was lucky and had no unexpected interruptions and was able to focus on my work and enjoy relaxing meals and conversation at the club. Next week, I'd have to be on my best behaviour.

Sophie made no demands. We had drinks at each other's sets and went to dinner a few times. People were used to seeing her at the places we went, and were unbothered, though walking around London with a celebrity would always attract some attention. One got used to the stares, whispers and nudges by the public, and the staff at our usual haunts were good at seating us discreetly and running interference if necessary.

It used to be that you'd see well known people going about their business as a matter of course – on the underground, in restaurants – even pubs – in shops, and in the audience of theatres. Actors, politicians, sports stars, and high profile businessmen could always be seen in taxi ranks, in local groceries and off licences.

Sophie's own limitations – had anyone been watching – would have provoked comment, or even amusement.

I never touched Sophie, in public or in private, leaving initiating that limited physical contact to her. She would sometimes take my hand walking down a street or hold it in a restaurant. These were random contacts, or done from some feeling that it was something she should be doing.

She'd act wholly based on her own feelings – or impulses – without regard to where she was or who was around. The consequence was that occasionally, she made the odd *paparazzo* rich. We'd both tolerate the following publicity. The press never knew who I was, which itself could be annoying. A few times I'd be mis-identified and the other party would sue the offending publication. If they were married, the damages could be considerable.

When Sophie first re-entered my life about a dozen years ago, it was often speculated that I was her father, uncle or sugar daddy.

"I act normally, and take your hand or impulsively hug you, but within a few seconds, I realise I can't sustain the contact," she once told me.

It upset her greatly, and she'd apologise. I could only remind her that she was guilty of nothing, but was the victim.

Such scenes would oscillate between the comic and the pathetic, but even in her more normal expressions of affection, I could never accuse her of being a tease.

I knew her too well to think she could get any further than innocent public contact. One day after a stage performance, she came by and was unusually tense. She stood with her back to me and asked if I could rub her shoulders. She was still in her forties at the time. I could feel her react the second my hands touched her. I gave two gentle rubs to relieve the muscles and she gave a short expression of pleasure. After the third repeat, she stepped away, said, "Thank you," and sat down.

It was her greatest wish to outgrow her sense of revulsion, but without professional help, there was no way she was going to. Nevertheless, she would go through many of the preliminary motions of ordinary seduction, like inviting herself back to my set for coffee, slipping off her shoes and curling up on my sofa and staring at me over her coffee cup. These were all moves from her stage and film work, sadly imitated in real life.

How deliberate or conscious this was, I didn't know. On stage and in films, it was very convincing.

She followed me up to my set on Friday night after dinner at Mon Plaisir.

"I've decided to start the drive to Lincolnshire Sunday morning, rather than the afternoon," I said, as I made coffee. "There will be less traffic and I don't want to take the motorway."

"I shall miss you," Sophie said.

"It's for less than a week," I replied. "You left *me* for two."

"That's different."

"How?"

"I wasn't spending time at the home of two attractive and eligible people."

This was the typical sort of ritual façade she would construct. It was not to be taken seriously. I never had any hint that Sophie harboured fantasies about anyone. The very idea would have filled her with horror. She was simply deploying her rehearsed repertory of "normal" behaviour, and I had accepted that I was part of that ruse.

I was her permanent excuse.

℃ℨ

My departure from London went like clockwork. I took a taxi from Albany to Southwark where I made several trips to my studio to move things into the lobby. At the appointed time, my rental car was delivered, and I was loaded and underway on schedule.

I wasn't in a hurry and drove over London Bridge and headed up the A10. There was less traffic, and for one who seldom drove and seldom left London, it was an interesting diversion that took me through an England I thought had ceased to exist. This was especially true after leaving the A10 and began meandering up the A1101.

I made better time than expected and was glad I had avoided the purgatory of the motorways.

I had booked into the Captain John Smith Hotel and managed to get a weekly rate. It wasn't a busy time for them, and they eventually accepted my request; mentioning a nearby Airbnb may have helped.

The Captain John Smith, like so much of modern life, was fake. While the façade, comprising four house fronts was real, it was clear that the whole building behind was modern. Inside, it failed to recreate Georgian proportions, details or materials, and low ceilings with basic coving and wall-to-wall carpeting covered the lobby from one set of windowed fire doors to the other.

At least the plumbing would be reliable.

I had what was pretentiously called an "executive room" which meant it had a large modern desk and convenient outlets and a broadband connection. Otherwise, it was soulless.

I telephoned April in the late afternoon, after I'd had a meal and a rest. I wanted to leave it late enough so that she wouldn't be tempted to invite me over before our scheduled time.

After telling me she was glad that I'd made it safely, she confirmed a ten o'clock arrival on Monday, then proceeded to give me directions.

"Your satnav probably won't be much good. Not only is cell coverage not brilliant, but there's no such place as Bickering anymore."

Of course not, I thought. All I have to do is go through the wardrobe, navigate Mirkwood, avoiding the slithy toves, turn left at Little Whinging, and the Emerald City would be right in front of me.

The directions were actually pretty simple, and I was able to trace the route on the Ordnance Survey map I had brought – already marked with pubs and interesting places I intended to visit.

I could see "Bickering Priory (site of)" marked on the map in the gothic font favoured by the War Office at some time in its history. Bickering Place was about a mile away and on a different road.

I'd had a late lunch in the busy hotel's carvery and didn't need supper. After a ritual flip through of about forty-five television channels and being tempted by none, I began reading the Courtauld's thick report.

As expected, the work was meticulous, well-presented and logically set out, moving from the general to the specific before backing away again for the conclusion.

I read the initial description and the table of contents before leafing through it to look at the photographs and graphs. The analysis was almost purely scientific with only the summary and conclusion offering an historical context detailing the way that Rembrandt was thought to have run his business. This section was lengthy, comprising about a fifth of the report. Individual experts and curators had contributed to it, but it was Dr Stirakis who pulled it all together.

There was nothing superficial about it, and while it didn't duck some hard questions like, was this the first or second version of the work, and how could have been unknown for so long, it did what a scientific examination should have done.

It even suggested that the Gardner's version should undergo "close and critical" scrutiny should it ever be recovered.

She put a powerful argument that the California version had undergone rigorous modern tests *twice,* whereas the Gardner version had not. Moreover, the place of connoisseurship and Berenson's place in that tradition had both declined in the intervening decades.

While I made many notes and annotations, the only thing I took issue with was, as Helena had said on Friday, the report only evaluated what it had found and made no comment about what it had not.

As mentioned, the fact that only one hand was evident had been reported but not questioned.

I thought a lot about this one. It was entirely possible that Rembrandt had, indeed, painted it all himself, but at an earlier date. In a variation of Sophie's theory, it may have been years or decades before someone (the man from

Porlock?) had seen and commissioned the portrait-format version.

It was a plausible scenario, but entirely without evidence.

Apart from the fact that the California version had been painted by a single hand, I had other objections of omission. For a week, the Courtauld experts had pored over the painting with magnifying glasses and bright lights and found not a single hair – sable or human – nor a smudge where one might have been removed. None of these things is uncommon in paintings from any period. Often, fingerprints are found, or smudges of them where fingers had been used to blend or create an effect. These could be quite distinctive, depending on the artist.

I'd email Beech about these speculations Monday evening, but for now, I returned Sophie's earlier email saying she hoped I had success, and was pleased to hear that I hadn't got lost and ended up in Somerset. She also told me she had arranged to see the first Invicta film Tuesday morning.

My email was in my traditional arms-length style. It suited me, and I knew that the tabloids had no scruples, though they tended to feed on the young and beautiful.

Chapter XV

I had done no more work – or thinking – about *The Storm on the Sea of Galilee* after sending Beech my notes and passed the rest of the evening with a murder mystery.

The Captain John Smith offered a good breakfast buffet that was open to the public and appeared to be well-patronised. When working, I'd often skip lunch, or just have a light one – unless there was a particularly good pub nearby.

After breakfast I had a chance to walk around Horncastle, get my bearings and see what it had to offer. I came across the offices of Stennett & Co., the estate agents where Marissa worked. Its premises, a shopfront in an indifferent building, attempted to look distinguished, but not off-putting. Judging by the properties in the window, being anything but egalitarian wasn't an option.

At around nine-thirty, I got into the car, and set off. It was only a dozen miles, but I wanted to leave a little time to get lost.

The map seemed clear with April's directions. Bickering Place was between Kingthorpe and Langton by Wragby. Signposts for Gautby and Wispington made me feel that I'd stumbled into an episode of *The Avengers* (no, not those Avengers, the *real* ones In Colour).

At more or less where April had indicated, there was a cluster of trees amid the fields and a gravel drive curving through ancient rhododendrons. It would be worth seeing even if it weren't the right house.

I don't know what I was expecting when I drove up in front of Bickering Place. Sophie hadn't told me much. I parked on the sweep and looked at the building. It was smaller than I had expected, though not small. What gave the house presence were the impeccable proportions which, almost Disneyland-like, tricked the viewer into thinking he was seeing what he was not. It was a trick that had been used in films for a century and still worked.

The house was modestly set with only a few steps up to the central front door. Three tall windows flanked the doorway on each side, and seven square windows of the same width were on the first floor. From my place on the drive, I couldn't see dormer windows tucked behind the parapet but expected they were there.

The foundations of the house were stone and looked to be late mediaeval or fifteenth century.

As I took my equipment out of the car, the front door opened and April Gilliat came to meet me.

"Sir Nigel, welcome!" she said, warmly.

She had the look of someone who had worked on a farm for decades and was well-educated to boot. She wore tweeds, a cardigan and sensible shoes. Sophie had told me that she looked like a character from an Aga saga, and it was an apt description.

"Would you like me to take this around to a rear entrance?" I asked.

You'd be surprised how many people say yes.

April laughed.

"What's Sophie been saying about me?"

She carried my paintbox while I brought in the easel and a drop cloth. I never dropped anything, but it made people feel more comfortable and sometimes, me, too.

"Why don't you pile your things there by the door, and then you can decide where you'd like to work."

As I looked around, I appreciated the architect's sleight of hand even more. The room had a low ceiling, not more than seven feet, and the long Georgian windows appeared to be French windows from inside, running from floor to ceiling.

Oak beams and a brick and stone fireplace confirmed that this was a Tudor house built on earlier foundations, then tarted up in the eighteenth century.

"Did you have any trouble finding us? I should have warned you that while there is no longer a Bickering, there is a Beckering not too far from here."

April led me through the ground floor. There was some nice furniture, but it was more modestly and sparsely furnished than I expected. The floors were wooden and covered with a variety of old and new oriental rugs. The main room had oak planks; the dining room, and kitchen had polished strips. I suspected that beneath these floors were ones of brick and stone. The wood may have been eighteenth century but could have been newer. The raised floor also accounted for the windows being so low.

Essentially, there were only four rooms on the ground floor. The main sitting room with a fireplace, a small study, and a square, formal dining room. A series of doorways provided two entrances to each room (the study's second door led outside).

The main room could hardly be called a sitting room, as, even with sofas, chairs, tables and lamps, it felt more like a place to entertain rather than relax *en famille*.

The master stroke of the eighteenth century renovation was the placement of a large hallway across the back of the building to accommodate the staircase in a single flight. What had been the original back of the house was now exposed Tudor brick and several filled in windows with low arches could be seen.

"Of course, all the brick had been plastered over to make a proper Georgian room," April said. "The removal had begun when we bought the house."

As fascinating as this was, the *piece de resistance* of the hallway was a large gothic window filled with clear leaded glass diamonds, supported with muntins. It had been placed centrally and, had the main room ceilings been higher, it would have been visible on entering the house.

I stood back to contemplate it. It had three lancets, and a pleasing tangle of *mouchettes* and *soufflets*.

"We did that," April said.

It would not have been an eighteenth century thing to have done – at least pre-Walpole.

"Titus found it when ploughing one day," she continued. "One of the stones has a great ding in it from the plough. You can see it from outside. Not all of it was there, of course, but only about six of the main pieces are new.

"The field was between where Bickering Hall and the priory were, so it could have come from either."

The window now looked onto ancient fields and hedgerows, just beginning to show a weak haze of green. April stood next to me looking out.

"Titus and I had a great debate about the glass," she said, in fond recollection. "We were both in two minds whether to have clear glass or tinted green, though we agreed on the diamond-shape.

"We decided to have the view of the seasons, but immediately opened a very small bank account to save for green glass should a developer fill the fields – which are not ours – with horrid biscuit-cutter 'starter homes.'"

April led me down the hall where a W.C. was secreted under the stairs and a doorway opened onto a large, modern conservatory.

"This is the South side and it makes the room useable all year."

We re-entered the house, walked the length of the hall again, and entered a large, fully modern, country kitchen – complete with Aga.

༚

April put the kettle on and I sat at the large wooden table.

"Marissa was showing a house this morning and should be here by eleven," she said. "I thought you could have a look around and see where you'd like to work and set the portrait. Sophie said you could set a painting one place and paint it in another."

"I can do that."

I stopped as April had just placed a plate of gingerbread squares on the table. I guessed that Sophie had told her of my liking for them.

"I can do things a number of ways," I resumed. "Ideally, I'd make the sketch in the actual place and take a few pictures as *aide memoires* for the light, colours and details."

I ate a piece of gingerbread while April poured coffee.

"Is this picture for an occasion? Birthday? Engagement? Miss Gilliat and I will need to discuss things like dress, hair and makeup, as well as pose: standing, sitting, casual or formal."

April laughed.

"Marissa will do whatever you tell her to," she said, amused that any discussion was needed.

While that attitude applied to children under ten, with anyone older, some discussion was needed to establish what was wanted.

Teenaged boys, usually indulging their parents or grandparents, could be won over with the inclusion of something of particular interest to them – a bit of sports equipment, a trophy, electronic equipment (though I warned them of being perceived as untrendy within two years), or sometimes a pet.

One lad brought me a photograph of his aquarium which I enlarged and stuck to my easel. I put it in the portrait and he helped me to get all the details right. It was painstaking work, but it transformed potentially difficult sittings into ones of satisfaction for both of us.

The lad is now a professor of marine biology and has the painting in his office.

At other times, there are serious ulterior motives to portraits. Holbein knew his place as an assistant marriage broker, and I, nearly five hundred years later, found myself in a similar position.

An Indian couple brought their fourteen-year-old daughter for me to paint. She had been contracted from birth to the heir of a good family in Calcutta, and this portrait had been requested by the boy's family, who was seventeen. When she was sixteen, Ella would be taken by her parents to her new life. It was a matter of tradition and honour.

In our conversation, during which Ella was present but silent, it became clear that both parents had become Westernised enough to resist this ancient tradition. However, they were religious, traditional, honourable and honest.

"It is a very sad situation, Sir Nigel," Mr Pandey said. "We could ask you to paint Nachelle like a disreputable woman, but that would not be honest, and there would be terrible gossip and our families in India would be disgraced. I could also ask you to paint her as ugly which would certainly put the young man off, but we cannot do that either."

As no agreement with me had been made, I was free to turn this commission down, but an idea had occurred to me while Mr Pandey was speaking.

"Would it be possible to speak with your daughter alone?" I asked. "Perhaps in the coffee shop across the street? You could be there, but out of earshot."

Mr Pandey looked stunned and was about to speak when his wife stood up.

"I think Sir Nigel has an idea that he wants to talk to Ella about."

Mr Pandey looked ready to resist when she continued.

"Sir Nigel has given us his time. He has put on a jacket and tie to meet us. His studio is clean and tidy. If we can be there watching, it should be safe."

"People might see him with her," Mr Pandey protested. "Then what might they think?"

"Very well," Mrs Pandey said. "Come. *We* will go to the coffee shop. Please bring Ella to us in twenty minutes, Sir Nigel."

Mr Pandey looked stunned but followed his wife out of the studio.

As for Ella, she remained in her place on the sofa, totally expressionless.

"Do you know this boy in India?"

"No."

"You don't write, email or text?"

"No."

"And how do you feel about this?" I asked.

"I want to go to university and study physics," she said, softly. "But if this is what my parents want, then I will do it. It's how they were married."

"What do you know about young boys in India?"

"I think they always want to be in charge," she said.

"I got the impression that your mother and father are more equal than that."

Her eyes came to life.

"They've been in England since I was born," and she gave the slightest of smiles.

"What was the name your father called you?"

"Nachelle. It's my real name. It means powerful."

"Let's go find your parents," I said.

Her mother came to all the sittings and supervised her dress, hair and makeup.

Ella wore a yellow *sari* with her hair up.

"They will be expecting to see a red *sari*," Mrs Pandey said. "It's the traditional colour for celebration and weddings. Yellow suggests intelligence and aspiration."

"Well, Nachelle," I said. "Let's show the world how powerful you are."

The result was the image of an attractive and intelligent young lady. She didn't look fierce, but she did look determined. Her pose suggested she was someone not to be trifled with, though even Ella thought she looked "hot" – a term that did not please her father, but made her mother laugh.

The family were delighted with the portrait and prayed that it would do the trick. It was rolled and shipped to India, and I feared I would hear nothing further. Then, one day, about a year later, as I left the studio, the three of them were waiting on the pavement.

"We have come to thank you," Mr Pandey said. "Your wonderful painting of Nachelle frightened the boy into telling his parents that there was a local girl he wanted to marry."

We went to the café.

"They sent the painting back and we have it hanging in our home," he said. "I keep telling Nachelle that that is the image she has to live up to!"

"And you?" I asked Ella.

"It's never nice for a girl to learn that someone doesn't want to marry her," she said, "but I have my GCSEs to help me get over it."

What was the agenda for Marissa? I wondered.

Chapter XVI

While April cleared the kitchen table, I wandered through the house taking pictures. There were a number of locations that would make excellent settings for a portrait. The windows in the dining room were particularly good for someone either standing or sitting, looking out.

There were some fine pieces of antique China and silver if Marissa wanted to contemplate or hold something. Then, there was the Gothic window and the receding fields. I could photograph them and paint her outside, too, if she wanted.

My fear was that she wouldn't want anything formal and want to be painted in her pyjamas lying on the green leather Chesterfield with a drink in one hand and a cigarette in the other.

Don't laugh. I painted a rock star's girlfriend that way in the 1970s.

Poor girl. The rock star ODed and his effects were auctioned for millions to his worldwide fans. When she married a Tory MP in the 1990s, they lived in constant fear that the painting would resurface. She tried to enlist my help in tracing it.

I decided that working in the conservatory would suit me, and with April's approval, moved my things in and set up my easel. While tightening the top bar to hold the canvas, I heard a car on the gravel sweep.

Even if Marissa were scary, I reflected that this was a lovely house, I had a comfortable room at the Captain John Smith, and April seemed to be as nice as Sophie said she was. There were pubs to go to, Lincoln to see, and the weather warming and the clocks having gone forward, it promised to be an enjoyable week. Bring it on!

As I stepped back from the easel, April appeared in the doorway.

"Sir Nigel, this is my daughter, Marissa."

ଊ

Have you ever sensed danger the moment you've met someone?

Maybe not danger, but great unease? That's the feeling that washed over me when Marissa came into view. The next thought that popped into my head was, "Elsie Palmer."

Sargent's curious portrait of a seventeen-year-old girl had always fascinated me. I knew a little of the story behind it: Sargent was a regular visitor to her mother's leased home in Kent where she entertained artists, writers and other interesting people. Elsie had not enjoyed the sittings, but got on well with Sargent and they remained friends until his death.

What I saw in Marissa – apart from a woman twenty years older – was a similar long auburn hair cut with a fringe, and eyes that looked at the outside world as if she understood nothing she saw, but everything within. She was very tall, five nine or ten (though it was hard to tell in her heels), and she had a memorable figure.

She approached me almost fearfully and extended her hand.

"Good morning, Sir Nigel. Welcome to Bickering Place."

She spoke as if she'd been given those words to say. Lincolnshire had provided an edge to her RP diction, though her intonation lacked nuance. (These were the sort of comments Sophie made to me all the time. I had come to regard them as theatrical critiques, not personal judgements.)

Then she turned and walked back to the doorway and her mother. It was hard to associate this childlike action with the successful businesswoman I understood her to be.

I made a sudden decision.

"The house is wonderful. Would you show me around the gardens?"

"I don't know much about gardens," she said.

"That gives us something in common," I said. I then turned to April, "We won't be long."

I moved to the front door so Marissa would have no choice but to follow.

I walked across the drive, straight from the front door to an expanse of lawn where I looked back at the house, trying not to stare at Marissa as she approached, but, of course, I wanted to see how she walked and moved. Before she joined me, I wandered across the grass to a place facing the corner of the dining room where it would be difficult to see us without getting close to the windows. Indeed, I saw movement in the room, but April stayed away from the windows.

Marissa walked up to me and seemed confident. She stood next to me – rather closer than one would stand to a stranger – and looked at the house with me.

"Did you know it was haunted?" she asked.

"I hadn't heard that," I said, intrigued.

I waited, but she said nothing.

"Do you live here?"

"That question is more loaded than you think," she said, and moved on around the side of the house where there were four small squares of garden with rose bushes.

"There used to be a large formal garden here," Marissa said. "The idea was that we would start with four squares and then add a few more squares each year, but other things came along and it's been like this for twenty years."

Moving towards the back of the house, there were deep borders along the rear wall filled with a variety of plants just planning to come back to life. The remnants of crocuses, daffodils and snow drops could be seen.

"There's a grove in the far corner and it has bluebells," she said, pointing to an area beyond the conservatory.

"Now, this painting I'm supposed to start this afternoon, do you have ideas of what you'd like it to look like."

She laughed as though I had said something very funny. It was a young girl's laugh, at odds with – well, everything.

"I want it to look like *me*!" she shouted with laughter and ran back into the house.

ఴ

I returned to the hotel by around five o'clock, having gone for a walk when I got back to Horncastle and picked up several bottles of tonic water and some lemons – I already had the gin.

Having had the kitchen give me a bucket of ice (I complained of a headache which could have been true), I threw my portfolio of sketches on the table and I mixed a large gin and tonic and dropped into the armchair.

This was going to be a long week. I took a deep drink and reached for the sketches. I had done about six full figure drawings in different places in the house. I had then drawn versions of her eyes, nose, ears and hands. This last set would be useful, but there was nothing of the other ones that were quite right.

I was gazing at the drawings, enjoying the gin and contemplating the events of the day when I was startled by my mobile ringing. I seldom used it as more than a camera and wasn't expecting to hear from Sophie this early.

She was eager to hear about my meeting with April and Marissa. I gave her a blow by blow description.

"The high point was a decent lunch," I said. "April prepared salads and sandwiches and a mug of good soup."

"No Aga sausages?"

"Not today," I laughed.

"April chattered and Marissa sat there and ate in silence while I tried to work out what to do next as the morning had accomplished nearly nothing. I contemplated escaping and fleeing back to London."

"Poor darling," Sophie laughed, obviously not taking things as seriously as I was.

"When we finished lunch, April turned to Marissa and said, 'Now, this afternoon Sir Nigel is going to want to work, so do whatever he asks you. He will want to see some of your clothes, so choose some things you might like to be painted in and bring them down for him to see.'"

"Does she always talk to her like that?" I asked, but didn't wait for an answer. "I told her to just bring three things down, and that she could get more if we needed them."

Sophie laughed again.

"I love it when you find yourself out of your comfort zone!" she exclaimed, still laughing. "I wish I was there to see!"

I was not yet seeing the funny side of things.

"I don't think you'd have liked that," I said. "I think April helped choose the clothes for Marissa, but they were all good for a painting. We were working in the conservatory, and she laid the clothes on a sofa.

"I told her to pick a dress and we'd walk around the house to see where it looked best and we'd work out a pose from there. I got the impression she thought this would be a splendid game. She seemed perfectly happy and cooperative."

I paused.

"I sense a 'but' coming up."

I laughed.

"That's nearer the truth than you know. She selected a dress and proceeded to strip off – right there – and put it on! As they say, I didn't know where to look."

"I bet you did," Sophie giggled, "and it was right where she wanted you to."

She kept giggling.

"Poor darling," she said. "After all that, I hope you found a good background and pose."

"I think we settled on a dress. The fifth one," I sighed.

When Sophie didn't say anything more – except stifle another fit of giggles – I finally asked:

"Is she all right?"

Sophie burst out laughing again.

"You tell me, darling. You've seen more of her in an afternoon than I did in a week! Sorry, I've got to go now. I'll call you tomorrow."

⁊

The day had nearly exhausted me. After finishing my drink and washing my face, I went down to dinner. I should have enjoyed it more as it was good. I thought it prudent to pass on the wine, but it would have made it even better.

Over dinner I had an idea. I knew that there were a number of studies of Elsie Palmer by Sargent, and there was even the odd photograph. If I could develop something effective playing on the Elsie Palmer look, the favoured dress and part of the house, all might not be lost.

I began an internet search and turned up a number of good photos of Queen Palmer at Ightham Mote along with various paintings and studies by Sargent, including several in preparation for the portrait.

Then, I found one I didn't know: it was a full length study with Elsie looking slightly to the painter's right. There was a fireplace behind her to the left and a dog at her feet.

It was a simple pose, elegant, unpretentious and with the figure in full light against a darker background, but it created a strong sense of presence. If Marissa stood like this at the foot of the staircase with the gothic window behind her and the newel post and the first two or three steps to her right, we'd have the making of an interesting story.

All I had to do now was paint it.

And keep my sanity.

Chapter XVII

Marissa met me on my arrival at ten. She was dressed in a white angora jumper and nicely fitting jeans. I tried to remember the last time I'd seen anyone wear an angora jumper. She was relaxed and welcoming, though she said little. I followed her into the kitchen where she handed me a mug of coffee before we moved into the conservatory.

"Mother's out shopping," she said, as she began her striptease to change into the dress we'd selected the day before.

I tried to ignore this and prepared my pallet and brushes. I squeezed out a large quantity of burnt umber, thinned it with linseed oil and roughly covered the white gesso. Using the edge of a pallet knife, I divided the canvas into approximate thirds, horizontally and vertically. This helped with the placement of the subject and background objects to create a balanced picture.

When I looked up from that, Marissa was standing next to my easel and staring at me. The impression of Elsie Palmer was very strong.

"Come with me," I said, and we walked into the hallway.

She followed me and watched as I looked around to see that things would fit into my idea.

"Can you please stand there at the bottom of the stairs," I said. "If this feels very awkward, tell me."

"It all feels strange," she said.

I smiled.

"Yes, it does," I said, hoping to sound reassuring. "Now, can you stand with your body facing that way."

I stood in front of her and held my hands out from her shoulders to frame the direction. She moved easily into the pose, but didn't take her eyes off mine. Since we stood only eight inches apart, this felt very awkward, for me at least.

I stepped back and tried to stand at the distance where my point of view would be. There was a problem in that the hall was too narrow and I couldn't step back far enough. I'd have to fudge it. I'd use photographs for the window and stairs, and I could paint her in the conservatory.

"That's it, thank you. Now, turn your head to face my hand."

I held my hand up about a foot from my head. She turned her head, and the pose was coming together.

"Good. Now, can you bring your right foot forward about six inches and point it towards me.

"Perfect."

I took a handful of photos in a patchwork since I couldn't fit them all in the frame.

"Now you can relax," I said. "I'm going to make a rough sketch on the canvas and then we can get to work. You can sit down, or get another coffee."

"Would you like one?"

I gave her my cup and she disappeared.

I placed her figure very nearly in the centre of the picture and roughly drew in the window and the staircase. I was able to get three full steps into the picture. It worked well. The oak newel post came up to just above her elbow, and its carved globe was interesting but unobtrusive. Painting all the window lead and the landscape behind it would be tedious, but I was pleased.

Marissa came back in and after handing me the mug, stood close to me, trying to make sense of the lines that meant much to me, not a lot to anyone else.

"For the rest of today, I want to build your figure. I'll have my photos printed when I get back to Horncastle and begin working on the background tomorrow.

I glanced around and moved a low coffee table.

"If you could stand there, we can get started," I said. "I'll try to give you a break in twenty minutes, but just ask me any time. You may talk if you want except when I'm painting your face."

Marissa moved to the place I'd indicated and took up the pose perfectly. So perfectly that it was unsettling.

"Now, Marissa, one final thing – and don't move until I tell you," I said. "I want you to imagine that you're a marionette. There is one string and it's coming right out the top of your head. I want you to imagine that the string is being gently pulled and it's lifting your whole body. Let it lift you as high as it can without being uncomfortable, and stay in that position. You can move now."

As with ninety percent of my standing subjects, she grew almost an inch.

"Don't be stiff, don't be uncomfortable. You did that perfectly," I said.

I started to paint. After two minutes, she suddenly spoke.

"That's me, you know," she said. "A marionette. I've always done what other people have told me."

I said nothing, and she reflected on what she said.

"I mean, I was never one at school who you'd tell to set off the fire alarm or do something dumb.

"I knew what was right, polite, safe and so on, and was happy to go along with it," she said.

More silence. Maybe a minute or two.

"To listen to my mother, you'd think I had been a juvenile delinquent."

I looked up at her and she smiled.

This was not a discussion to get into.

She talked about a few other things, mostly the house and the changes that had been made that she remembered. She was talking about the building of the conservatory when she suddenly stopped.

"You're painting the outside of my right thigh now, aren't you?"

It's not uncommon for sitters to have a curious "being touched" sensation when they're being painted, but it's vague, unspecific and non-invasive. The fact that I *was* painting the outside of Marissa's right thigh startled me.

At first, I ignored it, and then looked around the room to see if there was something reflecting my canvas well enough for her to play this trick. There was nothing; my easel was angled away from the direction of her gaze, so even if there had been a reflection, it would have been too oblique to see any detail.

Without a response, I put some paint on the right side of her neck.

"That's the right side of my neck," she said, with a coy smile. "And now, you're tickling my feet."

I was.

"Is this process bothering you?" I asked. "We don't have to do it."

"Don't worry, Sir Nigel, I'm not going to accuse you of doing anything inappropriate."

For the rest of the session, I worked on her hands and arms. I realised that when April returned, I would have to ask her to sit in on the sessions, and I didn't know the effect that would have on either of them.

Arranging a chaperone for a thirty-seven-year-old was well outside my comfort zone.

I looked at my watch. Marissa had been posing, almost completely still for forty minutes.

"You can take a break now and I'll tidy up some of the work," I said.

"May I see?"

"Of course, it's your portrait."

She came and stood next to me and looked.

The colour was still all burnt umber, but I had the placement and the rough outlines of the background. I was satisfied that her body was in proportion and I had begun shading to give her form. Her face was fully shaped, and her eyes and mouth well-defined.

"When I felt the brush strokes, I thought you might be painting in the French Academic tradition," she said, and gave me the same look.

In that tradition, all figures were first painted nude and then had clothes painted onto their bodies.

"And what do you know about French Academic painting?" I asked, more amused than provoked.

"Art History 'A' level," she said. "The class had fits of giggles when the teacher told us. We didn't believe him until we read it.

"One girl asked, 'Does that mean that all paintings of nudes are unfinished?'"

I'm afraid this struck me as funny as it did the girls, but, alas, apparently, not the art master.

"I never forgot that," Marissa said.

"Why don't you get something to eat," I said. "I'll keep working and leave early so I can get the prints made."

As she turned to go, I said, "Let me know if you can tell what I'm painting when you're out of the conservatory."

She laughed and went to the kitchen, and I resumed work.

A moment later, there was a girlish, rising scream.

"Oooh, Sir Nigel!" she called, with a cheeky inflection.

"No good, Marissa!" I called back. "I was painting the staircase!"

&

April came back shortly after we finished the sitting. She offered me lunch, but I declined.

"How are you getting on?" she asked, standing in the doorway to the conservatory.

I waved her in.

April made some expressions of approval. While Marissa was out of the room, I mentioned her sensations and suggested she might like to be present during the sittings.

"Do you think I don't have better things to do, Sir Nigel?" she retorted. "She's old enough to take care of herself, and she deserves whatever she gets."

A word about trusting me would have banished thoughts of tabloid headlines. I returned to talking about the painting.

"I think we've made good progress," I said. "Marissa seems to like it."

"Well, that doesn't matter. It's going to be a good painting; so whether *she* likes it or not is irrelevant."

Curiously, that odd statement resonated with the discussion I'd been having with Hawsley and Beech. Can a painting be good if no one likes it?

Okay, can it be good if no one sees it?

One can think too much.

I worked on my own until two o'clock when Marissa came back. She was carrying her dress and did her now customary undressing and dressing.

"Do you want to check my makeup?" she asked.

"That won't be important until we're nearly finished," I said. "There's no need to wear anything special at this stage, or anything you don't normally wear."

She resumed her pose. I was pleased to see she remembered the posture trick.

"That's one of the dilemmas girls face that men never have to worry about," she said.

I glanced up to show I was listening and that she should continue.

"If a girl is asked on a big date – a special dance, for example – she wants to look her best," she said. "But how much makeup can she put on before she frightens the bloke, or ends up looking nothing like the girl he asked out.

"I was a bridesmaid for a school friend – well, several school friends – but this one had a professional makeup artist do her for her wedding. There were several of us there. We each got a brush of blush and a smudge of mascara, but Peggy was unrecognisable.

"When she started down the aisle, the groom's face was one of horror, so by the time she reached him, it was all running with tears.

"The bridesmaids couldn't see her face, but we could tell by the look of the guests as she walked past them that something was wrong."

"Poor girl!" I said.

"Yes, the one day you want everything just right," she agreed.

"The vicar looked horrified at the bride in tears and the groom looking aghast, so his face also looked like a chamber of horrors."

I had stopped painting.

"Peggy turned and looked about to bolt when Craig grabbed her arm and pulled her back. He dragged her aside, wiped her face and whispered to her, and then they took centre stage again and all was well," she smiled. "It still is."

"Do you know what he said?"

"She told us a few months later. He said, 'Now you look like the girl I love.'"

I was moved, but perhaps Marissa had told the story so often that it made no impact.

I went back to work and she suddenly jumped.

"Ooh! That still hurts!" she exclaimed, holding her left side, just below her ribs.

Just as quickly, she resumed the pose and was quiet for twenty minutes.

We broke for coffee and she brought in a plate with more gingerbread.

"I'm going to work for another forty-five minutes or so, and I don't need you to pose," I said. "You can stay and watch, or go sell a house."

Marissa laughed.

"Things are quiet at the moment," she said. "They should be picking up – and did for a while – but people are afraid of losing their jobs, or are working from home and starting their own businesses."

All of a sudden, Marissa was sounding like a professional woman and not the tween she'd sounded like when we first met.

She sat in a chair behind me, relaxing with her coffee and a magazine, occasionally sneaking a piece of gingerbread. I got on with the work. The form of the figure was gaining mass and had reached the point where I had to give her a firm floor to stand on.

These descriptions may mean little to other portrait painters, but it's the way I think about it.

The first colour I put on the picture was the suggestion of the pattern in the oriental rug. Then I added a hint of shadow from the window.

Marissa was standing beside me now.

"All of a sudden, it has life," she said.

Chapter XVIII

It was a long way from life, but it had come on well. I had the colour prints made and enlarged one to A3 size, and went back to the hotel. I was planning to put my feet up when Sophie called.

"I know I'm early, darling, but James Beech has been trying to reach you," she said, urgently. "He had to get my number from Bill and Virginia. You really should give people your mobile number."

It was a familiar plea, though Sophie was almost never used as my answering service.

"I'd better call him then," I said.

"No wait," Sophie said. "I saw *Devonshire Street* today, the Invicta film. It was a bit creaky, but not bad."

"Did you find the Rembrandt?"

"No. Well, I found *a* Rembrandt. I asked to have a few frames printed. I'll have them for you when you get home."

"Was there a – "

"I'm seeing *Mignon* tomorrow – the Invicta film, not the opera," she said, quickly. "You'd better call Inspector Beech."

Why did women either never finish a conversation or keep it going too long?

Beech could wait. I was going to close my eyes for half an hour. . .

℘

After supper, I called Beech.

"Have you read the Courtauld report?" he asked, without preamble.

"Most of it."

"Read the pigment analysis and compare the reports," he said.

"I can do that this evening," I said.

"When are you coming back?"

"I was going to come back Friday."

"Can you make it Thursday?" he asked.

His tone was his most professional and sounded more like an instruction than a question.

"Why?"

"Hawsley called me this afternoon. An unknown Monet was brought in to a Brooke & Sons' affiliate auction house in Vienna."

He paused so I could take it in then said:

"I'm meeting Hawsley at Mount Street Gardens at ten on Friday."

"I'll be there."

Well, there goes the visit to Lincoln.

With luck – and no theatrics – I could get Marissa's face and maybe her hands to the point where the portrait could be finished in the studio. It would mean working a few hours longer tomorrow, but I could do that if things progressed as well as they had today. I had to admit that getting away from Marissa Gilliat a day early and getting back to London was an attractive proposition.

Yet, the more urgent thing on my mind was Beech's instruction to look at the paint analysis in the Courtauld report.

There were several pages of tables and graphs showing chemical composition followed by a comment about each of the colours of the pallet. All the paints used in the California *Storm* could be found on other Rembrandts, and there were no outliers.

I turned to the report from Weisman & Rossi. I was trying to find the charts when I remembered that Hawsley had had the tables reformatted to match Gwilym Jones & Stottlemeyer's report on the Steen. Checking my copy, I found the sheets of the reformatted data tucked into the back of the Courtauld report.

With the two sets of data side by side, it didn't take long to find the anomaly that had caught Beech's eye.

Our conversation with Hawsley on Friday would be very interesting.

ॐ

I packed my car on Thursday morning. The hotel wanted to charge me the normal nightly rate for the four nights I had stayed, but I pointed out that the agreed weekly rate was less. When the young assistant manager balked, I told him that if he filled the room I had paid for on Thursday, Friday or Saturday nights, he'd have to pay me for the room was technically mine.

At Bickering Place, April was disappointed that I wouldn't be there on Friday, but she was happy with what I had done, and delighted when she saw there was very little left to do. Marissa gave no indication of either disappointment or delight in my leaving early.

I had my photographs of the hallway with me and was able to fill in much of the background detail, making the picture look more complete than it actually was.

April brought me a coffee and sat watching me paint, occasionally talking about Sophie, or the house. I'd been working for about twenty minutes when Marissa came in, carrying her dress and shoes. She took off her jeans and shirt, and put on her dress, shoes and took the pose.

"Aren't you going to brush your hair?" her mother demanded, rather angrily, ignoring the fact that Marissa had stripped down to her bra and knickers.

"Nigel's already painted it," she said, not raising her voice or sounding irritated. "He says it's never exactly the same way twice, so he paints it once and that's it."

"*Nigel*?!" April asked, sharply. "When did you get on such familiar terms? I wouldn't dream of calling him Nigel unless he asked me to, and even then, I'd find it difficult."

I had no intention of entering this discussion and kept painting.

The exchange went on for about fifteen minutes and had moved on to other subjects, like why she wasn't wearing any jewellery, considering the nice pieces she had?

"Nigel and I discussed all this before we started," Marissa replied, still speaking in her unflustered schoolgirl voice.

"Again with the 'Nigel.'"

I just kept mixing the paint and putting it on the canvas. I thought it was coming together and had the makings of a pretty good painting.

I worked through lunch. At least the kitchen was far enough away so I couldn't hear any arguments.

Marissa's part was just about finished except for the eyes. I wanted to give them some life, and lift her above the Elsie Palmer stare, but I had not seen any real life in them since my arrival. Even when disputing with her mother, her eyes remained flat. It was one of those instances where a single highlight would transform the whole picture. That's the way it had been with my first portrait. I had painted my late wife and by the purest accident captured her eyes, and that was the start of my career.

Apart from the eyes, I just had to decide how impressionistic I wanted to leave the background. As both the staircase and the window were handsome, I thought some detail was appropriate. It would have been more modern to leave them vague.

I had about an hour before I wanted to leave when Marissa and April came back from lunch. The low level bickering continued until I thought a bit of artistic temperament was called for.

"April, will you please leave. I have less than an hour to capture your daughter's face, otherwise I shall have to club her and drag her by the hair back to London."

Both women were stunned into silence. When she recovered, April stood.

"I am so sorry, Sir Nigel. I will let you work in peace," she said, with forced calmness.

Marissa hadn't budged from her pose.

"Clubbed and dragged by the hair?" she exclaimed, with a laugh. "Actually, I might quite like that."

"Focus!"

ꞓꝾ

We managed to finish the sitting without interruption, argument, clubbing or hair-pulling. Frustratingly, I hadn't got the eyes the way I wanted, but I had some sketches that might help once back in London and away from Nightmare Abbey.

I took all the supplies out first, then the easel, and finally the portrait. It was wet, but with care, there would be no serious damage.

I went to the kitchen to thank April for her hospitality, apologise for leaving early and for telling her to leave.

"I'm sorry," she said. "You were quite right to ask me to leave; she was the one you were here to paint."

I thought this was generous because earlier I had asked her to be present.

"I'll let you know when the picture is finished and dry enough for you to collect," I said.

"Or, I could deliver it," I felt compelled to add, against my better judgement.

They came to the front door to say goodbye and both gave me a brief hug. I walked across the sweep to my car and Marissa followed. She startled me by taking my hand as soon as we descended the steps.

I glanced back to see April's reaction, but the doorway was empty. I got into the car, but before closing the door, I said:

"You never told me who haunts the house."

"Can't you guess?" she asked, with a look I hadn't seen all week. "*I do*."

Her answer chilled me, but that feeling was eclipsed by one of satisfaction as that brief flash in her eyes was all I needed to complete the portrait.

Chapter IXX

I couldn't remember the last time I had so many things to talk to Sophie about. In the event, it was several hours after my arrival before I was able to sit and chat with her.

She met me outside the studio and helped me move my clobber back in. I didn't try to hide the portrait from her. Why would I? I was very pleased with it, especially now I knew what I could do with her eyes. Sophie appeared to like it, too, but had the sense not to comment more than, "That's coming along well," until it was finished.

She came with me as I returned the car, then I asked her what she'd like to do next.

"You must be exhausted," she said.

"I could do with a drink and good meal," I said. "There are lots of places around here."

"I know where you can get a good *steak au poivre*, a decent gin and tonic, and one of your favourite wines," she said.

And so, after dropping my things in my chambers, I went to her set.

Sophie was in a good mood and chatted happily as she finished preparing our food.

Although bursting to bring her up to date in the Gilliat madness, she had news, too, and I let her go first.

"I told you I'd seen *Devonshire Street*," she began. "Well, I saw *Mignon* yesterday. *Mignon* had a very French feel about it which isn't surprising as it was directed by one of the refugee French Jews who was able to make it out. The trouble with it was that it moved like a French film: lots of time spent on details that only the French are interested in – like a man buttoning his shirt and tying his tie – but there was no Rembrandt there. However, Marcus gave me the prints from *Devonshire Street* today and I'll show you after supper."

We were now seated and eating.

"You've done well," I said.

"I'm seeing *Escape to Brioni* tomorrow," she said. "It's the last of the Invicta pictures that Beckman worked on."

"This steak is perfect," I said, "and so is the wine."

"Chateau Giscours is one of your favourites, isn't it?" she asked.

"You're looking pleased with yourself. You've got other news," I said. "Come on, what is it?"

"I've got a part in the new Tom Stoppard play," she said, with a big smile.

I congratulated and toasted her. I was certain it would run and run which meant that Sophie would remain in London. I know I am betraying the same possessiveness that I've attributed to her, but the closeness of familiar people is part of being human.

"Rehearsals start in May," she said. "I can't say anything, but the cast is going to be very good. New names and some old friends."

We talked about the schedule, the proposed production at the Noel Coward Theatre and the character Sophie would play.

This delayed any discussion of Bickering Place until Sophie gave me a mug of coffee.

"'Bickering' is the right name for that house," I said. "Is Marissa mad? She did and said all manner of curious things."

Sophie looked at me sadly.

"I can't see where you get that idea," she said.

"No, I don't think you can. I told you Marissa changed her clothes in front of me – in the conservatory – of her own home! April was there when she did it today. Then, she took my hand when I walked to my car."

"April?" Sophie asked, mischievously.

I glared at her.

Sophie had started giggling when I began my story and was laughing loudly now.

"Am I going to have to scratch her eyes out?" she asked, still laughing.

"Is that normal?" I demanded, but that didn't stop Sophie's mirth.

"Oh, darling. Couldn't you see? It's April who's mad."

☙

Sophie said this as though it was something so obvious that I should have seen it from the start. The revelation – if Sophie was right – stunned me, and I began to replay my visit to Bickering Place and still failed to pick up any clues.

"When April's husband died, he left everything to Marissa," Sophie said. "Titus knew April wouldn't know what to do."

"But April seemed normal, and Marissa the fruitcake," I protested. "Marissa was the one who said the odd things, has the unsettling stare, stood uncomfortably close, and undressed in front of me."

"Which did you find more abnormal: Marissa undressing or April not saying anything?"

"I think they're both bats," I said.

"Still, you appear to have got a good portrait done," she said. "May I see it when it's finished?"

That was the main thing – I had done the portrait and I had high hopes for its completion. If it came out as well as I hoped, it could be my second entry for the Summer Exhibition.

"Why has Marissa never married?" I asked. "I also wonder about her ability to hold a job. I would have thought she'd freak-out colleagues, unless what I saw was some bizarre charade."

"She's a very pretty young lady," Sophie said. "She'd be a great person for a feature in *Country Life* or *Country Living*. Can't you see her elegantly showing the journalist through the house?"

"She certainly has presence," I said. "Her height – especially in her heels – is impressive, and while she has young country woman features, she doesn't have the outdoor look."

"Oh, didn't you get to see her in her wellies?" Sophie asked, with a giggle. "She's the sort of girl who still has her last school uniform."

"Stop it!" I exclaimed, then returned to my earlier question, trying to get Sophie to be serious.

"So, no notable men?" I asked. "And, she lives at home? Has she always? I can imagine her living in a nice apartment in Horncastle with a husband she never told her parents about."

Sophie was laughing hard now.

"Darling, you were the one who spent a week there," she chided. "Why didn't you ask? You get your sitters to tell you all sorts of things."

We were still sitting at the table, and she cleared all but our coffee mugs, which she refilled.

"I suppose you'll just have to go back to Bickering Place to get your answers," she said, then added, teasing. "But, I bet you will find that Miss Gilliat will find an

191

excuse to come to London before you invite her for Varnishing Day."

"I don't think she could wait until I left, but she was the most cooperative sitter I ever had. I almost never had to remind her of her pose, and she'd stand there uncomplaining for longer than just about anyone I've painted."

"Including me?"

"Most definitely including you."

Sophie went to her desk and brought back a large envelope and sat at the table again, but on my right rather than opposite.

"These are the stills from *Devonshire Street*," she said. "I didn't see any paintings in *Mignon*. That one was pretty turgid."

She opened the envelope and passed me the black and white photographs.

"The story is about the life of a house in Devonshire Street," Sophie explained. "How what had been a large town house for a wealthy family had been sold and converted into flats, and as time passed, the occupants of the flats changed and became poorer and poorer and the building declined."

One of the pictures that illustrated this decline was the removal of a painting from a wall in a grand hallway. In the first picture, I couldn't tell what it was, but in subsequent pictures, it was turned towards the camera.

"*Belshazzar's Feast!*" I exclaimed, and turned the print so the painting was correctly oriented.

I looked at Sophie who had her cat and cream look.

"Look at the next ones," she said.

Later pictures showed the painting placed on the floor and someone turns it around and leans it against the wall, showing the back.

"I'll be right back!" I said, and rushed to my set.

I was able to find what I was looking for quickly and was back with Sophie in about five minutes.

I opened the Courtauld report and found the photographs that showed the back of *The Storm on the Sea of Galilee*. I had brought my magnifying glass and checked the photo from *Devonshire Street*. After checking back and forth, I passed her the report and the glass.

"What do you see?" I asked.

She looked puzzled for a moment, then took the magnifying glass and looked back and forth at the two images.

After a minute of checking and rechecking, she looked up.

"The backs of the paintings are identical. All the labels are in the same place," she said, surprised. "What does it mean?"

"I wish I knew."

Chapter XX

Sophie and I talked until nearly one, by which time I was frightening myself about forgers, Marissa and April, and Bickering Place.

While I told her much about what I'd been thinking regarding the mystery of the paintings, I did not mention what I believed Beech had discovered, nor did I mention the Monet that had turned up in Vienna.

I hoped I could get a good night's sleep and be on top of things in the morning when I met Hawsley and Beech, but at least I now had something significant to tell them.

ᔥ

I did manage to sleep deeply and dreamlessly and, fortified with a good breakfast, I walked to Mount Street Gardens and found Hawsley settling himself into a quiet corner where there would be enough privacy for our discussion.

Beech followed me in a few minutes and without preamble, Beech began.

"After reading the Courtauld report, I went back to compare its chemical findings with those done in California," he said.

"Yes," Hawsley said, "they were the same."

"That's the point," Beech said. "They were *exactly* the same, down to two decimal points. There was no variation whatsoever."

I couldn't tell if Hawsley didn't get it, or just didn't want to.

"It is highly improbable that the equipment is identical in both places," I said. "It is *more* improbable that their calibrations would be so close as to reproduce identical results across the whole pallet."

Beech nodded.

"So what does it mean?" Hawsley asked.

Beech and I looked at each other to see who'd speak first. I nodded to him, if only so that Hawsley felt he was getting good value from him.

"At present, I can think of only one possibility, albeit with two variations," he said, sounding as though he was giving evidence. "Either, the Courtauld copied the California report, or the California team copied the Courtauld in some convoluted conspiracy."

"I don't want to believe that of the Courtauld," Hawsley said, firmly.

"We don't either," Beech said. "Given the number of people involved at the Courtauld – and presumably in California – it would be a very difficult ruse to pull off."

"There is at least one other possibility," I said, tentatively.

Both men looked at me.

"That the two micro-spectroscopy machines used share the same database," I said. "It would take some clever programming, but it could be done."

Beech was considering this when Hawsley interrupted his thoughts.

"Really? That easily?" he asked.

"Piece of cake," Beech replied, distractedly, and returned to his train of thought.

"If a paint in a certain range was being tested, it would display a pre-determined result?" Beech mused. "Clever."

"It's more likely that a chemical marker is in all the pigments and it forces the desired result," I said.

"Wouldn't the markers have been detected?" Hawsley asked.

"Of course, but before displaying the result, its presence would be automatically suppressed," I said.

"Bloody hell!" Beech exclaimed.

Hawsley was struggling to keep up and looked worried. Beech turned to him.

"I'm sorry, Sir John, but it looks like there is a conspiracy here, but who is complicit, we can't yet tell."

He proceeded to repeat what Beech and I had said, to ensure his understanding.

"So the Rembrandt is probably a fake?" he asked, gloomily.

"Almost certainly," I said, remembering the photographs I'd brought. "Here's some more evidence that what we're dealing with is fraud."

Beech leaned forward as I produced the pictures from *Devonshire Street* and the Courtauld's report.

"The labels on the back of the *Belshazzar's Feast* and those on the back of *The Storm on the Sea of Galilee* are identical," I said. "Not only identical, but in exactly the same positions. The stretcher and frame are the same, but the image is not."

"This is too elaborate," Hawsley said. "Too improbable."

"What would you expect an authenticated, recently discovered Rembrandt to sell for, Sir John?"

"Well, *The Unconscious Patient* was discovered in 2020 and most recently sold for about four million dollars," he said. "The record was in 2009 for a portrait that went for eighteen million pounds – so for this, between twenty and thirty million dollars."

"Plenty of cash to go around," Beech said.

We sat in semi-confused silence. I was considering how any of this could be proved, Beech was probably a few steps ahead of me, and Hawsley was, no doubt, contemplating his losses – both financially and reputationally.

"At present, this is just a theory," Hawsley began.

"Yes," Beech said. "But the evidence is looking strong."

"I agree," Hawsley said. "Can I swear you to silence, at least for the moment?"

Beech seemed about to speak.

"It's all right. I'm not going to ask you to do anything illegal or not to report anything illegal," Hawsley said. "There is a lot of money at stake, but more importantly, there are the reputations of everyone who has handled this picture – and the Steen, and now, the Monet, which we haven't discussed yet. While I'd like to see the guilty hanged, drawn and quartered, I don't want innocent reputations to be destroyed.

"I need to think about this," Hawsley continued, wearily. "One thing, if the database is compromised, how can we find out what we're dealing with?"

"Do the analysis the old-fashioned way – by hand," I said. "The question is, is there anyone who can do that?"

∞

In fact, a phone call from Beech to his successor at Scotland Yard, followed by a phone call from the Yard to the National Gallery to the Department of Chemistry at Imperial College, identified a PhD student able and willing to undertake the work with the proviso that when everything was declassified, she had the rights to writing the scientific papers.

Hawsley wasn't happy with the picture being moved again.

"Where's the painting now?" Beech asked.

"We moved it from the Courtauld to our warehouse in Nine Elms," Hawsley replied.

"*That* neighbourhood's changed a bit!" I exclaimed.

Since the Covent Garden fruit, vegetable and flower markets moved from central London, Nine Elms had been an area of intense residential and commercial development with the former Battersea Power Station, American Embassy and new underground station transforming the area.

"Our lease still has seven years to go," Hawsley said, with a smile. "We're already looking for something comparable, but nothing close is available for what we want to pay."

"Have you tried Milton Keynes?" Beech asked, sardonically.

"We've even looked further than that," Hawsley said. "Anyway, the Rembrandt has now been moved to Imperial, and we have to trust them to keep it safe."

Hawsley's expression told me that he knew more than he was saying.

These arrangements had been made over the weekend, and the three of us agreed to meet again on Monday at the club to formulate a strategy on the Rembrandt. We needed to decide what to tell the

Rijksmuseum by way of alerting them to the situation and suggesting they carry out an independent manual analysis of the Steen; see if anything useful could be leveraged from the discovery of the labels on the frame and stretcher, and finally, discuss the Monet, of which Beech and I had yet to learn anything.

There was also the matter of finishing Marissa's portrait.

I felt that my ability to contribute to this project was waning and thought I should excuse myself sooner rather than later. As things evolved, I didn't get a chance that day.

On Monday, Beech and Hawsley were already in deep discussion over coffee when I arrived. I was on time, and coupled with my doubts about my usefulness, suspected they had conspired to meet earlier.

"Sir John was just telling me that he's already advised the Rijksmuseum to get an independent, manual test," Beech said, as I joined them.

"How did they react to that?"

Hawsley gave an ironic smile.

"They were not delighted, but at the same time, they were grateful," he said. "They asked me to keep them in the loop on the other pictures."

"Do you think they'll re-test it?" I asked.

Hawsley raised his hand in a 'who knows?' gesture.

"I don't care. I've done my bit."

He looked about to continue, but then bowed his head and stared at his coffee.

"You do appreciate what a disaster this can be for the art world, don't you?" he asked, when he looked up. "This has the potential of destroying the market. Remove the trust, and it will collapse."

Hawsley's voice had a note a desperation about it that underlined the magnitude of what we thought we'd discovered – and it was still a matter of our own instinct, curatorial sense and deduction.

"What I wonder," I said, breaking the silence, "is how it is that we seem to be the only ones who smell a rat?"

There was a pause as my coffee was delivered.

Beech was the one to answer.

"Because we're the only ones to question what we're told."

Neither Hawsley nor I commented, so Beech continued.

"We haven't given due consideration to the evidence of the pictures from the film," he said. "Nice work, getting those, by the way. Well done to Miss Gordon.

"What this suggests is that the actual canvas and frame were reused by the more recent forger. How and why the X-ray, IR or UV photographs didn't show anything, we can only conjecture. My guess would be that the image of *Belshazzar's Feast* was removed – either chemically, or mechanically – and the *Storm* painting constructed on the canvas."

"Are we sure it's an old canvas?" I asked.

"We're back to the databases," Beech said. "It would be easy enough to impregnate markers in the canvas that would give whatever result was wanted."

"But we have no proof of that," Hawsley said, defensively.

"When does the new analyst expect a result?" I asked.

Hawsley shook his head.

"Everything should be ready in a fortnight or so," he said. "All the tests that were done with electronic equipment will be done by traditional methods. The graduate student is a Russian chemist called Nadezhda Bellman. She'll be receiving her PhD this year. She's enlisted – with my agreement – two other PhDs to cover the additional areas we're concerned about.

"And, by the way, the Courtauld doesn't know we're doing this," he said.

"That gives us time to consider the Monet, about which you have told us very little," Beech said.

"I don't know much. A chap in our office in Vienna – Winkler – got wind of it through an old friend at another auction house," Hawsley said. "Winkler was one of the few in the loop about the Steen and the Rembrandt, so when this friend told him of an unknown Monet turning up – well, it set his antennae twitching.

"At the moment, that's all I know," he continued. "Winkler hasn't seen it; it's gone for tests, and he hasn't been given a clue as to its size or the period in Monet's life. The likelihood is that it's Nazi plunder and not part of our problem. We'll just have to wait and see. The good news is that Winkler has been promised an early look at it.

"I told him to say nothing about the Steen and Rembrandt, and I am certain he won't."

"Let's hope it's not connected to our painting," I said.

The club was filling up with people for pre-lunch drinks. Hawsley invited me to stay and join them for a drink and lunch, but I wanted to get back to my portrait of Marissa and excused myself.

Chapter XXI

It was comforting to be back in my studio. I placed Marissa on my large wooden easel and put the collapsible one away, along with the paint box that I travel with. The bottles of turpentine, linseed oil and cobalt dryer were returned to their shelves. I opened the window, took out my sketchbook and made coffee.

Before leaving Horncastle, I had done several sketches of that look that Marissa had given me and planned how I could capture it in paint.

I had plenty of time to do it, make mistakes, scrape it off and try again. That's not the sort of technique one wants to use in front of sitters, but a necessary step more often than you might think.

I began with the easier things to get back into the mood and style of the picture. The window, the staircase, a large mahogany table against the wall and the rug all needed finishing. Halfway through the afternoon, I decided that the table needed a vase of flowers on it for balance and colour. I painted a tall waisted crystal vase with some tiger lilies. I knew Marissa's birthday to be in mid-May, so they would be appropriate.

I'm not into astrology or monthly flowers, gemstones, and other things dreamt up by marketers in order to sell something, but the odd symbol that relates to the sitter is useful and can fill an empty space. It also gives the critics something to talk about when they can't think of anything else.

With the work on the window, the stairs and the flowers on the table, I had suggested a fairly complete but soft-focus background that made the figure of Marissa stand out, as though she was about to step forward and out of the canvas.

I replaced the portrait on my easel with an oil paper tablet and copied the pencil sketches made in Horncastle in paint and colour. It took a few tries, but the fewer attempts made on the canvas, the better. Finally, I could put it off no longer and made the changes on the painting.

The result was that I had captured that look she'd given me, but I wasn't immediately certain that it fitted the portrait I had painted.

I turned the easel so I could see it from my armchair where I sat with a magazine to "surprise" it from time to time. I'd only been there for about five minutes when my entry buzzer rang.

I answered the intercom with a simple, "Yes," as it wasn't beyond the local youths to entertain themselves pushing buttons, but it was Sophie. I buzzed her in, put the door on latch and looked for the sherry bottle.

She tapped on the door before entering.

"Is everyone decent?" she called in her best theatrical voice.

"I was just at the Film Theatre and – bloody hell!"

She walked slowly towards the portrait, eyes wide.

She scanned the picture, considering the details, but kept being drawn back to the face.

"I thought *my* portrait was unsettling, but this – "

She changed her position to look at it from different angles.

"What *did* you two get up to?"

I laughed, but Sophie turned to me.

"I'm serious," she said, sternly. "If that's the way she looked at you, she has *intentions*."

I laughed again.

"*You* couldn't stop laughing over dinner," I reminded her.

"Poor Nigel," she said. "You really have no idea, do you?"

It was something she said to me on a regular basis, but today she sounded more severe.

I handed her a glass of sherry.

"Don't you like it?" I asked, feigning hurt.

"That doesn't matter," she said. "When she sees this, Marissa will either kill you or drag you to Tahiti."

I could see there was nothing further to get from this conversation and sat down.

"What did you come here for?" I asked, drinking my sherry.

Sophie turned away from the picture and sat in a corner of the sofa, instantly slipping off her shoes and tucking her feet under her, as she had done when she first visited my studio.

"I've been to the Film Theatre to see the last of the Invicta pictures Beckman worked on," she said. "*Escape to Brioni* is a curious piece, neither one thing nor the other. It was part romance, part intrigue, and part surreal with random things happening. For example, in the middle of a heated argument in an office between the hero and his employer, carnations began falling from the ceiling. They carried on their fight, not paying any attention to them and after the man stomped out, there was a shot of the boss left in the office, but without a sign of a carnation.

"Anyway, the sets were stylised with painted windows, curtains, bookshelves, mirrors and paintings," she continued. "When the hero and heroine finally get together, they head to Southampton and get on a ship for Brioni. The final shot shows them on deck, on a real ship, looking happy and approaching Brioni. That thirty seconds is in full colour, too."

"Southampton?" I asked. "Wasn't this filmed in Hollywood?"

"Well, you didn't see Southampton, it was just a wall of a pier with a gangway up to the wall of a ship," Sophie laughed. "I expect Brioni was Catalina.

"Anyway, no Rembrandt – or anyone else."

I collected the empty sherry glasses and coffee mug, made sure the caps were back on my paints, dried the brushes and secured the turps and linseed oil before getting my coat from the bedroom.

Sophie was staring at the portrait when I came back into the main room.

She still looked displeased.

"What's bothering you, Sophie?"

She looked at me, then back at the picture.

"Damn it! I'm jealous!" she said. "Irrationally jealous – this is one of the best things I've seen you do.

"I think I'd better be here when you show it to her."

ⳍ

The next morning, the portrait of Marissa was in my cupboard for works in progress and I was beginning work on a recently appointed judge. Painting judges was relatively easy. Essentially, it was just face and hands. The robes required a certain facility or knack. As long as the details were accurate they were secondary to the human features. The challenge for me was to create an interesting and personal background. It was seldom possible to paint them in their homes, but I could work from photographs of rooms and objects.

This M'lud was about as boring as you can get. He was a bachelor and appeared to have no interests beyond the law. I gave up on trying to get him to speak after about ten minutes. He posed pompously and woodenly. At one point I was tempted to put in some *sgrafitti* to indicate strings from above, attached to his head and hands, but the customer is always the customer.

Still, he didn't undress in front of me or stand too close.

He seemed pleased after the first sitting, shook my hand and gave me a surprisingly warm smile.

"Thank you for not asking impertinent questions or talking drivel for two hours," he said.

One might expect him to be more open during subsequent sittings.

I didn't.

He wasn't.

୧

When I got back to Albany, there was a note from Hawsley.

"Good news and bad news. I'll be at the club, J" it read.

I arrived at Mount Street Gardens shortly after six. Hawsley was standing by the bar, and after I ordered a drink, we moved to a quieter area. That was the first day that I noted that Hawsley was looking older, clearly stressed by the possible collapse of the whole art market and his two century-old family business.

"How's the Lincolnshire portrait?" he asked.

"I finished it today," I said, proudly. "With luck, you can see it at the Summer Exhibition."

"Friends of Miss Gordon weren't they?"

"Mad as hatters – nice house though," I said. "Georgian overhaul of a Tudor *maison de maître*. Well done."

"I had a call from Vienna this morning," Hawsley began. "Someone found the Monet on a list of Nazi plunder."

"That's a relief!" I said. "But what took so long?"

"Good question. Apparently, there was considerable – shall we say – *opportunism* when the lists of plundered works were being compiled after the war. 'Aunt Gertrude had a big painting. I can remember seeing it as a child. Looking back, I think it was by Monet. . .'" Hawsley theorised. "There were a lot of suspected claims and those lists were only consulted after the 'more serious' claims were investigated. Eventually, as the reclamations dwindled, the existence of the secondary lists was forgotten."

"Plausible."

"Some scholar or graduate student happened on them in an archive and brought them to the attention of one of the museums," he said. "A relatively minor employee at the auction house was a friend of the academic and reported it. It then took a while to trace everything back.

"The claimant is long dead – heirless – but the description given at the time was conclusive enough to establish a sort of provenance."

"As good as coming from a film studio," I said.

"Now, don't go and spoil it all," Hawsley said, concealing his irritation well. "Nevertheless, Beech should add it to the list of things he's looking into."

While Hawsley paused to drink his coffee, I told him of Sophie's latest findings from watching *Escape to Brioni*.

"It's good to have that angle nailed down," Hawsley said. "Please thank her for me."

"And the bad news?"

Hawsley looked bewildered.

"An unknown Modigliani," he said, quietly.

I waited for more details.

"Found in South Africa," he added. "It's on its way to Paris for examination and testing."

"Has any preliminary work been done?"

Hawsley chuckled.

"Well, this time they checked *all* the plundered art records," he said. "Nothing turned up. It's an unusual painting, I am told. Supposedly, it's a view from the room Modigliani is believed to have lived in when he first moved to Paris.

"Exactly where the painting was done is unclear, and the house and surrounding buildings are not thought to be there any more, or are much changed," he continued.

"Well, we know what 'going to Paris' means," I said. "I think it's safe to consider this one not your problem."

Hawsley laughed.

"Yes, it will be interesting to see what some other unsuspecting bastards make of it," he said. "Still, I think you, Beech and I should keep an eye on it. After all, we know of two dubious pictures, we don't know who else might be dealing with similar rogue finds."

"The irony is that no one else is going to be more open about it than we are," I said. "The best course is the one we would never take: buy a page in the *Times* saying, 'Information wanted about any recently discovered unknown paintings by masters.'"

"Chaos."

"What I haven't worked out is whether that sort of thing would be in the perpetrator's interests or not," I said. "The scam might work best if it's kept under wraps."

Hawsley thought a moment.

"Well, it's certainly better for Brooke & Sons."

Chapter XXII

It was certainly fortunate – and also remarkable – that word of the Rembrandt and Steen hadn't leaked out, but it was still early days. What usually happened was that there would be a lot of noise in the popular press, and the experts and institutes would keep quiet pending tests, investigations and evidence.

Even if there were an eventual judgement one way or the other on a painting, people would continue to believe what they first thought or heard. Popular myth is easier to believe, never mind that Lizzie Borden was found not guilty, or that the Sacco and Vanzetti judge was exonerated by two inquiries, or that – despite what the Beefeaters tell you – about half a dozen men successfully escaped from the Tower of London.

It is curious that it is in the art market that the "truth" is seemingly more important than in other areas of commercial life, but that does not explain why fifty per cent of everything sold at auction is fake.

My own collection of pictures is not large, though I do find difficulty in finding wall space for anything new. I have very few old pictures. For all my involvement in the *Storm* in the tea cup of the "rediscovered

Rembrandt," I am more comfortable with the scientific data, the numbers and the probability of its veracity.

My own collection is mostly of living artists – or ones who were alive when I bought their pictures. The older pictures are etchings or engravings printed many million times.

They all have two things in common: first, I like them. I like seeing them every day. Secondly, I didn't buy any of them with the idea of making money.

Just as one should never buy a house for oneself on the expectation that it rises in value, neither should paintings be bought for their investment potential. People who do that tend to be collecting autographs, not aesthetic experiences.

This is one of the problems with portrait paintings. The picture – no matter how good – is about the person, not the artist. That is its value: the old, much beloved headmaster who still presides in the school's hall; the company's founder who led and built the organisation and supported countless people; the victorious admiral who was a tough bastard, but had some amusing quirks. But, as time passes and everyone who knew them dies, and memories fade, the original purpose and value of the portrait diminishes. It's just one of a row of similar people, like stamps in an album.

Yet, each of those portraits had been thought out, designed and painted to reflect that person. At worst, the company closes and its furnishings auctioned or tossed in the fire. At best, the old headmaster becomes a target for peas catapulted from spoons by successive decades of students. The admiral? Well, new admirals come along and he's moved along the wall until there is no space and he follows his predecessors into retirement in the basement.

If a dozen or so of my paintings survive my death by a hundred years, I'll be happy.

൙

Things went back to normal for about two weeks. With the longer days, Sophie and I would enjoy a walk in the evening light. Sometimes it would just be around Berkley Square, or into Green Park or a wander in Shepherd Market.

Sophie had some film work coming up and would be moving to a hotel near Pinewood – at the expense of the production company – until her part of the filming was over. She didn't tell me much about the film except that it was a murder mystery based on a successful West End play.

"Not *The Mousetrap*," she said, before I could comment.

I'd finished painting the judge and was working on two more portraits, but I kept the pace leisurely and spent time in the studio clearing out old sketches, throwing out forgotten dried out paint tubes and the other clutter that can accumulate.

When not working or cleaning, I'd read but not before putting the portrait of Marissa on the easel and looking at it. While I added a bit of colour to the background here and there to balance the picture, I didn't touch Marissa's figure. I decided it was finished and called April to tell her.

"Marissa will be delighted!" she exclaimed. "She was very excited about the whole project once you started work. I'll leave it to her to contact you and agree when to see it."

I explained that I could still make adjustments. That didn't seem to matter to April. She said Marissa wanted to go shopping and visit some old friends and, according to April, she was dying to see it.

April said she'd pay the balance of the commission once she heard from Marissa that all was to her satisfaction, and then she asked about Sophie. It was a friendly conversation and I had the feeling that we both could continue chatting unless I drew things to a close.

"Tell Marissa that I look forward to seeing her again at her convenience," I said, and then said goodbye.

I didn't ask April about exhibiting it in the Summer Exhibition. I thought I could ask Marissa when she came, after all, it was her image that would go on show.

I told Sophie about our conversation, and while she was glad it went well, she added:

"If either of them comes on her own, be careful," but I couldn't get her to elaborate.

∞

Several days later, I had a note (sent to my studio) from Marissa on what looked like scrap paper kept by the telephone, with, "I'll be in London next week and will call at your studio at three o'clock Wednesday. Love, Marissa," scrawled on it.

I reflected on the ephemeral nature of education – even good, private education – before marking the date in my diary. My vanity hoped for a bit more enthusiasm, but I have learned that in this day of telling and showing strangers everything about your life, sincerity is an early casualty. So, it seems, are manners.

My bruised ego didn't have time to enjoy itself because almost as soon as I read the note, the telephone rang.

"Can you meet me at the club, Nigel," Hawsley asked, breathlessly.

"I can be there within the hour," I said.

"Good," he said, curtly, and hung up.

∞

It was only half an hour on the Jubilee Line, so I made it in plenty of time without rushing. Hawsley looked like he'd just arrived and was flushed, but he'd had time to get a large glass of iced water.

Things must be serious.

As it was early, I had tea. When it came, Hawsley looked around and leaned forward.

"The balloon's going to go up," he whispered. "Somehow the lid has stayed on this long, but news has come in from our offices and contacts at other houses – "

My face may have betrayed a too casual attitude to his serious statement.

"Listen, Nigel, this is bloody serious!" he nearly spat. "In the past forty-eight hours, an unknown Pissarro turned up in Tokyo, a Thomas Lawrence in Vancouver, a Pimenov in Miami, and a Holbein – *a Holbein* – in Mumbai!

"How the hell does a Holbein get to Mumbai?" he asked, nearly in his normal voice. "Not a single one of them previously known. If any one of these is authenticated, it will open the floodgates and the whole art market will collapse."

"Well, it's credibility will," I said. "And – you are assuming that all are fake. Be careful, Joe Duveen got into expensive trouble over such things.

"On the upside, with the collapse of name collecting, people will have to buy pictures they actually like," I added.

"Don't you care if people start forging your paintings wholesale?"

I was about to answer but Hawsley interrupted.

"No, bad example," he said, unapologetically. "No one is going to forge your pictures. Banksy, for example."

"Could anyone tell?" I asked. "How about a fake squashed cat by Damian Hurst?"

"Damn it, why aren't you taking this seriously?" Hawsley nearly shouted.

Heads turned. He gave a slight wave to the room and sat back.

"Why aren't you taking this seriously?" he asked, in a hissed whisper.

"Because, Jack, this means it's no longer our problem," I said, and ventured a smile.

"You and I and Beech no longer have to solve this," I continued. "In fact, you have the chance to be something of a hero. You, Sir John Hawsley, of the renowned and respected firm of Brooke & Sons, have the first full documentation of one of the suspect paintings and have worked with a former Scotland Yard Art and Antiquities Unit Chief Inspector. Right now, *you* know more about this than anyone in the world.

"Go back to Dover Street, call up Scotland Yard and Interpol and the FBI unit and offer your services," I said, with real enthusiasm. "Get Beech on board and decide exactly what you want to tell them.

"You've probably got all the puzzle pieces except who is doing it," I said, urging him to move.

His face suddenly changed.

"Yes, of course! I see it!" he said, as things fell into place.

"Don't worry, you're not ruined," I said, and he looked at me, uncertain as to whether I was teasing.

Chapter XXIII

I was dying to tell Sophie that our little project with the Rembrandt was about to explode into an international sensation, but needed to keep quiet about it until it hit the news.

When she came over that evening, she knew something was up. All I could do was say that I'd tell her as soon as I could. She accepted that. She knew the importance of confidentiality and secrets, but was still curious.

We were about to go for our walk and were at the door when my phone rang. It was Hawsley. Sophie waited patiently in the sitting room while I took the call in the study. There was no door, so I knew she'd hear everything, but decided it didn't matter.

"I've just spoken to Beech," Hawsley said. "He's going to come around and join a call with several of the auction houses, the Yard and Interpol. We understand the database hacking, but how are the pictures being painted?"

"Many known paintings by masters have been scanned in very high resolution," I said. "Whoever is doing this has access to scans of the painters he's forging.

"Next, someone creates a new image – like the Steen crowd scene or the *Storm in the Sea of Galilee*. Objects from known works can be rotated, altered or distorted to make a new picture. The new, fake, image is scanned and an algorithm with Rembrandt, Steen, Lawrence or whoever's brushwork style is programmed into the file. *This is why every brushstroke on the Rembrandt looks like it was painted by him.* It also explains the absence of finger marks, hairs and other evidence of a human presence.

"It is then printed, probably on a large flat-bed inkjet printer using a set of pigments, thickeners, drying agents and other chemicals that will as near as damn it match the paint in use in the desired time period.

"The grime, dirt and dust – as well as the aged varnish effect – are probably done using nanotechnology.

"Do you understand?" I asked.

"No, but I can repeat that," Hawsley said.

"I reckon you're looking for a bunch of boffins who are expert in nanochemistry, image manipulation and artificial intelligence, but Beech is the one to help with the criminal profiling."

Sophie had unashamedly moved closer to the door and was listening intently.

"Now, remember, this is our theory based on the evidence from one painting," I said. "It is a theory – but you already have a head start with the manual paint analysis you're having done. The results of that should help prove the theory."

"You should explain this," he said.

"No, you have the necessary clout in the art world and with Beech there to back up the evidence and the theory, you're the one to do it."

There was silence at the end of the line.

"Thank you," he said, eventually. "I'll keep you in the loop."

∾

Sophie and I went to the open spaces of Green Park where we could talk.

"Is this as important as it sounds?" she asked.

"More than either of us can imagine," I said.

We walked through pools of golden light and listened to the bustle of Piccadilly and the traffic around Hyde Park Corner.

"It's good to see so many people just enjoying the evening," Sophie said. "There are those rushing about, but look how many are here just to enjoy it."

We walked a few hundred yards in silence.

"I heard from Marissa today," I said. "She's coming on Wednesday around three. Would you like to be there?"

"Wednesday? No, I can't," she said. "That would have been a good idea. Would your friend Beech be available? Or Bill?"

She was laughing, but there was an edge to it.

଼

I was pleased with the portrait and had latterly thought of entering it into the Royal Society of Portrait Painters' Summer Exhibition, rather than the R.A.'s.

In preparation for Marissa's arrival, I put the painting into a temporary frame, placed it on the easel and covered it with a blue velvet cloth. A bit of drama never goes amiss, and since the sitter already has a very good idea of what the picture looks like, surprising it like this is a way of seeing it fresh.

While waiting for Marissa, I made notes in my sketch book about what we knew and didn't know about the fake paintings that were appearing. While I was reasonably certain about how the pictures were created, I was less sure about the mechanics of creating the designs for them, or how the convincing collection of dust and debris was fabricated for the canvas backs.

The buzzer sounded just after three o'clock. I released the latch and opened the door to the landing. I'd already put out some champagne flutes and retrieved the bottle from the refrigerator as I waited for the elevator to deliver Marissa.

She tapped lightly on the door before entering. Sophie would have been pleased to see her description of Marissa so fully embodied. She *did* look like she'd stepped from the pages of a magazine. She wore a sage green overcoat, a faux suede skirt and a blue cable knit jersey over a neatly ironed denim shirt. Her hair hung loosely and she wore a minimum of makeup yet she still gave me that same Elsie Palmer impression.

Her face broke into a big smile when she saw me.

"Sir Nigel!" she exclaimed, and ran forward and hugged me. "See, I've remembered my manners," she said, girlishly, "and addressed you properly."

We exchanged a few words about her mother and Sophie, and then she looked at the velvet covering over the picture.

"Is that it? Is it really finished?" she asked, eagerly.

"I think it is," I said. "But the reason you're here is to agree with me, or ask for changes.

"If it is finished," I began, "I'd like your permission to exhibit it over the course of the summer."

I told her about the two exhibitions I had in mind.

Her face lit up.

"That would be wonderful! Yes, of course!" she exclaimed. "Would I be able to come see it?"

"Bring all your friends," I said, then moved toward the easel.

"When can I actually have it?" she asked.

"The summer exhibitions run through August, so any time after that."

"And if I want it now?"

"I can have it wrapped and delivered within a week," I said. "But, I would like to exhibit it."

She nodded, and her eyes shifted to the covered canvas.

"I don't want to keep you in suspense," I said.

I gently pulled the cloth from the picture, watching her face as I did so.

Her eyes widened and her mouth opened. Tears appeared in her eyes and she took a tentative step towards the picture, then looked at me.

"How *could* you?" she shouted, then repeated very softly, "How could you?"

I was so surprised that I looked at the picture to see if anything had happened to it.

"I can't believe you could do that! It was supposed to be a secret!"

With that, she turned and rushed from the studio.

℘

I was not going to chase Marissa across Southwark, and I was too rattled to remain at the studio. I took a long look at the portrait and couldn't see what she'd objected to, then took it off the easel and slipped it into the storage rack. I put the champagne back in the refrigerator and closed up.

Though not yet cocktail time, once back in my chambers, I poured myself a brandy and waited for Sophie to return.

By the time Sophie came over shortly before eight, I had run the gauntlet from depression to anger and had settled in confusion. I was convinced that the portrait was good and had concluded that Sophie was wrong: April was fine, Marissa was the one out to lunch.

Sophie had opened a small shopping precinct in Whetstone.

"It doesn't win me another BAFTA, but it's good PR – or so my agent says," she laughed. "The people were nice enough. It was low key, which suited me.

"The only trouble was that I couldn't buy anything – if I bought from one shop, I'd have to buy from all of them."

Sophie was not a conspicuous consumer. She lived amazingly simply and had not let her set fill up with bits and pieces. She had a few ornaments and a limited number of clothes – for an actress.

I anticipated the next things she was going to say and began making her a gin and tonic. She told me about some of the people that had spoken to her.

"Talking to fans is a reality check," she said. "When they are my age, it's not always comfortable facing that reality.

"Cheers," she said.

She took a breath after she drank, and then sat down. In an instant, her shoes were off and her feet tucked under her.

"So, talking of fans, how did you get on with the wonderful Marissa?"

I took a mouthful of G&T and told her.

Sophie kept her eyes on me the whole time. I left nothing out.

"Oh, the poor girl!" she exclaimed, when I finished.

I don't know what reaction I'd been expecting, but it wasn't that. Sophie ignored whatever expression I made.

"And you didn't follow her?" she demanded, in disbelief. "You just let her go like that?"

"I wasn't going to chase her. How would that look?" I retorted.

"It would look like you cared!"

Chapter XXIV

O nce again, Sophie's view of things had rendered me speechless and even more confused than I had been. When I was finally able to speak again, all I could do was ask if she was hungry.

We went to the club, being the easiest and most private option. I was feeling bruised, and Sophie had her fill of fans asking her questions and having scraps of paper pushed at her for autographs.

On the way in, I saw Hawsley at the bar with colleagues from Brooke & Sons. After seating Sophie, I went for a quick word with him. He saw me coming and detached himself from them and walked to me.

"How much does Miss Gordon know about our little problem?" he asked.

"Quite a lot about the Rembrandt, little about the Steen and nothing about the others," I said.

"Good," he said. "This crowd knows nothing about anything. I'm going to be here for a while. May I join you for coffee?"

Sophie was intrigued when I told her.

"I offered to take you home after dinner and then come back, but he said he was happy to have you here. He also said I could fill you in on the bits you don't know."

"Does that mean you've been keeping more things from me, darling?" she asked, but it was a tease. "Do I get a badge?"

I was happy to fill her in as it kept the subject of Marissa at bay. I told her of the tests, the identical chemical analyses, and the surfacing of the latest masters around the world.

"How does the picture in *Devonshire Street* fit in?" she asked. "All the right labels, but the wrong Rembrandt?"

"I have no idea," I said. "I can only guess that it was seen as a good canvas to paint – or print – the new image on. Maybe the forger works in a Hollywood props department."

"What does the Courtauld think of your theory?" she asked, again identifying an obvious gap in the story.

"They don't know," I said. "The idea to get an independent assessment was Beech's. Both he and Hawsley tried to find someone to do it, and I think they wanted to keep the Courtauld out of it."

We enjoyed our meal and a small dessert, and when we'd finished, I went to find Hawsley.

"The spring is always a busy time for us," Hawsley said, after greeting Sophie. "The team deserves a treat, so I bring them here for drinks."

"Nigel tells me you have a basic understanding of our sensation in the making, Miss Gordon."

"Please call me Sophie."

"Most people call me Jack. Nigel calls me Hawsley which I think comes from his Royal Navy days addressing other ranks."

Hawsley was relaxed and charming company. He took things at face value, didn't pry or make innuendoes about Sophie and our opaque relationship. Sophie was engaging and careful not to give any indication that we were other than old friends.

"There are things I want to tell you," Hawsley said to me. "The report on the Rembrandt is nearly ready. It's being presented on Monday at a lab at Imperial at ten. Can you make it? Beech will be there."

"I wouldn't miss it," I said. "I was one of the ones who set the hare running, so I deserve to be there when it turns out to be a real Rembrandt."

"Does Nigel have trouble taking other things seriously?" Hawsley asked Sophie.

"I'm used to it," she replied. "I know it can be hard on others, but I've known him since I was fourteen."

I was tempted to kick her under the table.

"I'll give him this," Hawsley began, "he made me realise I'd nothing to worry about: if it's a real Rembrandt, we'll get the commission and fees; if it's not, then our reputation will be saved, which is worth just as much."

"I think that's what Nigel calls 'Jesuitical thinking'," Sophie said, laughing.

Hawsley gave me the time and location of the presentation.

"You are more than welcome, too, Miss – Sophie," he added.

"Thank you, but I have a meeting with my agent," she said. "That's probably best for all concerned."

Hawsley grew serious.

"I heard more today," he said, gravely. "A Soutine in Milan, a Sassoferrato in Moscow, and a Bronzino in Cairo."

The rate of appearances was accelerating which meant that containing the news was now impossible.

"Two things, Jack," I said. "First, on Monday you will know if the Rembrandt is fake. If the Rembrandt is fake, then the veracity of the others can be challenged. They will be tested rigorously and it will be up to Beech's successors to catch the bad guys. Secondly, have you noticed that none of the paintings has been found in its home territory? Their placement is designed to take time between discovery and expert evaluation."

"Surely some of those cities have experts," Sophie protested.

"Indeed, they do," Hawsley replied. "However, their expertise on such paintings goes as far as, 'This is convincing enough for me to refer it to an expert on Soutine' – or whoever.

"A Soutine in Milan and a Bronzino in Cairo? Nigel's right," he continued. "It's designed to create time for rumour and sensation to pollute opinion.

"They must be flooding now because it's been kept quiet so far," he mused.

"They are forcing the issue with a coordinated dumping of pictures," I said. "Unfortunately, the quantity suggests that these have become relatively easy to make."

We sat in silence considering what these things meant.

Hawsley stood.

"Thank you both for your wise counsel," he said. "I'll see you Monday. I wish it were sooner."

Walking home, Sophie reviewed what had been said and asked a number of questions.

When we arrived at Albany, I attempted to guide her to her door, but she resisted.

"I'm accepting your offer of another coffee and a brandy," she said, steering me towards my set.

"You didn't think we'd finished talking about Marissa, did you?"

ларов

It wasn't late, and I had no good excuse to refuse. It would have only been a postponement anyway.

A sudden flash of inspiration provided me with an effective tactical manoeuvre.

"You haven't seen the portrait since I finished it," I began. "Come to the studio tomorrow morning and you can judge for yourself whether Marissa had any grounds for her reaction."

Sophie was about to tell me that there was no point in delaying discussion when her curiosity got the better of her.

"Fine!" she almost snapped. "I'll come at eleven and you're mine until after lunch."

It's the perennial problem of being friends with actors: you never know if the lines they are speaking are their own. In spite of her displeasure. Sophie gave me a light kiss in the middle of Rope Walk (no doubt there's a by-law against it) and went inside.

I supposed it was part of the battle of the sexes: given Marissa's outburst, a man wants to forget it and move on. From his point of view, it's over and cannot be changed. From a woman's point of view, the incident is a starting point for extensive discussion and exploration. It becomes a deconstructionist exercise that can go on indefinitely and suck all sort of previous male behaviour into it until there's nothing left but emotional wreckage.

The irony that at the end of the dissection, there is not an iota of difference in the original incident or its consequences, is not noticed.

I was confident that Sophie would find nothing amiss in Marissa's portrait. Nevertheless, I could use the intervening time to plan damage limitation and shorten the duration of any recriminations.

ℬ

I went to the studio at the usual time on Thursday, put Marissa's portrait back in the frame and on the easel. I covered it with the velvet cloth to give Sophie the same experience Marissa had. Once that was done, I made coffee and read the latest edition of *Apollo*.

Sophie arrived with an armload of red tulips, and after greeting me, found a vase under the sink and arranged them.

"You should always have flowers here," she said. "It's all so sterile. Flowers make people feel at ease."

I handed her a mug of coffee.

"This is the way things were when Marissa came," I said, and ran through what I remembered of our preliminary chat.

"What was she wearing?"

I told her.

"Did she look good?" Sophie asked.

"Yes. She looked very nice."

"Did you tell her?"

"No. Of course not," I said. "I can't think she'd welcome comments about her appearance from a geriatric."

Sophie made a disapproving face.

"There was champagne and glasses on the counter," I said. "I'm sure she saw them."

"I expect she did," Sophie said, her eyes on the easel.

"Then you will also note that the combination of a flattering old man and a bottle of champagne could be misconstrued."

"Hmm," Sophie said, but whether it was agreement or scepticism, I couldn't tell.

"Marissa was standing there," I said, pointing to a medallion on the rug. Sophie moved to it.

"I then unveiled the picture. Marissa was silent for a moment, then screamed at me."

Sophie stared at the portrait and said nothing. I stood there holding the cloth, waiting.

"You didn't change much since I saw it," she said. "The eyes and few background details. It looks richer."

"That's all," I said.

She moved a few steps to the left and right to see if it changed the effect.

"The eyes follow you," she said.

"It's not a difficult effect."

She backed away to view it from a distance.

"It loses none of its impact," she said. "It fairly screams across the room."

Then, Sophie picked up her coffee and sat down.

I folded the cloth and put it away and sat down, too. Neither of us said anything and continued to stare at the picture.

Sophie broke the silence.

"I still think it's one of your best paintings," she said. "It has amazing presence and the staircase, window, table and rug are great – impressionistic, but rich in detail.

"As for Marissa, she looks amazing," she said, admiringly. "Who do you think she's in love with?"

Chapter XXV

How was I supposed to know the answer to that? Fortunately, Sophie's schedule kept her busy until Saturday evening when she came around with an invitation to supper.

I should say that apart from Sophie's infrequent but generous parties, I was the only one to visit her set. When I went over, no one else was ever there. She said it was one of the ways she could separate Sophie Gregg from Ligeia Gordon.

Over the years, I learned many of the differences between the two. The main difference is that Sophie Gregg is very shy and insecure while Ligeia Gordon is gregarious and confident.

"I know a lot of people 'fake it until they make it'," she once told me, "but I can't do it."

While Ligeia Gordon could be switched on instantly, when Sophie Gregg re-emerged, she was always affected, sometimes shaken.

Sophie was sensitive, though not overly. She cared for her friends – both in and out of the theatre. One of the things I knew bothered her was that Ligeia was generous – and seen to be generous – usually to encourage others to be. This left Sophie without the ability to be generous as a private person.

It was not a separation that I could fully understand, and it could appear arbitrary. I had to remember that I was dealing with someone continuing to deal with at least one life-changing trauma.

Saturday supper was very low-key. Sophie made a simple *salada tricolor* and a *cacio e peppe*. She'd also found a bottle of Lacryma Christi.

During supper, she kept up a monologue of the two charity events she'd been to. Friday had been a fund-raising ball, and Saturday a lunch and visit to a home for children. As she had recently narrated a popular cartoon, she spent much of the afternoon telling stories in that character.

"You've probably never seen them, but I can sketch four animals quickly for children's autographs," she said. "A cat, a dog, a mouse and a camel."

"A camel?"

"Well, I was trying to do a horse, but they evolved into camels," she giggled. "Anyway, the children like them."

She cleared the plates and presently I heard the espresso pot gurgling. She put the small white cup and saucer before me.

"Have you given Marissa further thought?" she asked.

For a moment, I affected my helpless man expression, then said:

"As a matter of fact, I have," I said.

Sophie registered the desired surprise.

"I checked my bank account online this morning and saw that April had paid the balance due on the portrait. It's paid in full. Commission, hotel, food and car hire."

"Did you think she wouldn't pay?"

"She agreed to pay if Marissa was happy with the picture," I said.

Sophie looked as confused as I had been after discovering the payment.

"So, she liked it," Sophie said, almost as a question.

"Later yesterday, I had a call from April," I said, and Sophie sat up and stared intently at me.

"She said that Marissa thought the painting was 'unbelievable,' 'amazing,' and that she'd 'never imagined looking like that,' but it was exactly how she felt," I related, hardly believing it myself. "April rambled on with other paraphrases, most of which were disjointed, but were things like, 'I wonder who else sees me this way,' and that I saw something no one else had."

I confess to thinking of her undressing in the conservatory when April said that, but didn't tell Sophie.

"April wants to see it herself before it's exhibited," I said. "She wanted to come down Monday, but I told her we were both busy, but Tuesday would be fine. If you'd like to be at the studio, she's going to try to be there by eleven."

"Is Marissa coming, too?" Sophie asked.

I must have looked terrified because Sophie laughed.

"Don't worry, I'll be there, but I can't promise to protect you before the painting."

⌘

The weekend passed normally until Sunday evening when I was wading through the last of the Sunday papers. There was a writer whose weekly article I enjoyed. He wrote one of those diary columns that reviewed the week with wry comments. Three lines caught my eye:

> Those familiar with the workings of an institution recognise the signs when something big is about to happen. The sudden arrival of all the top – present and past – people from Scotland Yard's Art and Antiquities Unit in London at the end of the week has not escaped the notice of friends in the art world. Has there been a heist that's not been reported, or are they here to advise the BBC on some new programme?

It could be either of those things, but I was reasonably certain that the writer knew that the inferences of a major theft were wholly speculative and that this looked more like the BBC PR department at work.

Those in senior positions in the commercial art world and in the museums knew the A&A unit officers well. If one of them had met a detective in a "police pub," then a gathering of more than the usual number would be noticed.

There were innocent explanations for such a gathering – retirement parties, awards ceremonies, or significant promotions – but the notion that Beech had gathered his former colleagues seemed the most likely reason to me.

I cut out the article and put it with the notebook that I'd be taking with me to Imperial College in the morning.

Chapter XXVI

I'd never been to Imperial College, so I left plenty of time to find the laboratory where the presentation would be. I had nothing to show that I was entitled to be there, and in these days of multi-layered security, I was half expecting to be refused admission.

The laboratory was tucked in the maze behind the main buildings. Inside, there was a porter's area where coats, umbrellas and parcels could be left. I gave my name and the room number.

The porter, who fit the standard types for porters all over academic Britain, consulted his log.

"The lift is near the end of the corridor on the right, Sir Nigel. Fifth floor, then turn left."

I was expecting him to add, "Someone turned right once and hasn't been seen since." It was that sort of building.

I found five-thirteen without mishap, knocked on the door and entered. Beech was already there, and after exchanging pleasantries, I gave him the clipping.

"I had a phone call about this yesterday but haven't seen it," he said, reading it.

"Were you behind the summoning of the team?" I asked.

He offered to return the cutting, but I told him to keep it.

"Even though I'm retired, you don't suppose I have complete operational freedom, do you?" he asked. "I've kept the chief informed from the start. There's been no action as there is only one suspect painting in the country, and I've had eyes on that."

I can't say I was completely surprised, but it hadn't occurred to me. Our little investigation was suddenly looking a lot bigger.

"Fortunately, the conclusions in the article are just wrong enough to divert attention," Beech said.

Hawsley had just arrived and caught what Beech said.

"A narrow escape, indeed," he said. "How much longer can the lid be kept on?"

"A lot depends on the motives of the perpetrators," Beech replied. "It could be a disruptive anarchist organisation using sophisticated guerrilla tactics to crash the art market. If that's the case, the countdown is underway and there will be a tsunami of publicity.

"A second scenario is that there is a blackmail aspect. Most likely, these would be terrorists wanting a *lot* of money and crashing a major market is a bonus," he continued. "If this is the case, we can expect a ransom demand along the lines of, 'Give us five hundred billion dollars or we'll dump more undetectable fakes on the market and tell the world which paintings in every museum and major collection are fake.'"

Hawsley was not looking well.

"For good measure, they might name the dealers and auction houses who authenticated and sold them.

"A third possibility is that it's just a prank," Beech said, more lightly. "One to prove that the emperor isn't wearing any clothes and that science and technology can do anything a human can.

"The drawback to this scenario is that it's long, complicated and very expensive. It's hard to see a bunch of graduate students pulling it off – unless – " Beech broke off, "*unless they have backing* from the first or second groups."

"None of these is good," Hawsley said, sadly.

"There is a fourth possibility," I said.

Beech and Hawsley looked at me.

"I've said it before," I said. "It's that we're wrong and the pictures *are* genuine. Someone came across a cache of pictures and sent them around the world to control the publicity and achieve better prices as individual pieces in different markets."

A door at the rear of the laboratory opened and two young men and a woman entered. They were informally dressed and didn't wear lab coats.

We sat at one of the benches. Two of the men went to a door in the corner marked "Storeroom" and wheeled out a dolly with a crate on it and the woman held four thick bound reports.

I chuckled to myself when I saw that the crate was wrapped with high-visibility warning tape reading, "Danger Radioactive Material." In the right storeroom, this wouldn't attract notice and no one would mess with it.

We watched as it was manhandled onto the front bench and the painting unpacked.

Hawsley was visibly holding his breath. For a Rembrandt to be moved by anyone other than professional art handlers was rare. I was telling myself that they knew it was a fake, so the handling wasn't a major concern, but it was still a lovely painting.

Using an assortment of poles, clamps, grips and other equipment designed to hold test tubes, retorts, Erlenmeyer flasks, funnels, burettes and other laboratory equipment, the painting was secured where it could be seen by all of us.

The one carrying the reports appeared to be the leader, and when all was in order, faced us.

"Sir John, gentlemen. I'm Nadezhda Bellman, an organic chemist awaiting my *viva voce*. Through mutual acquaintances, Sir John commissioned me to look at this picture and analyse the paint."

She spoke with little accent, and her presence suggested experience of lecturing.

"This was about as blind a test as it could be: I know nothing about art; I had not heard of Sir John when I was given his name after completing the report, and I have no contacts – and have had no contact – with any museums, galleries or auction houses," she said, pre-empting a lot of questions.

"This is Jonathan Beale, a recently appointed lecturer here who specialises in nanotechnology," Bellman explained. "His work has been mostly in the behaviour of fluids."

She turned to the third man.

"This is our dustman, Dr Jean Carrel," she said, and got a chuckle from all of us. "He analysed the canvas, dust and pollen on the canvas and that tucked between the stretcher and the canvas."

Bellman made an expression.

"I had to learn a lot of new terminology for this: art, pollen and dust. It's all in the report," she said with a laugh. "You will forgive me if I explain what is obvious to you. I do not wish to teach you to vacuum eggs."

We glanced at each other.

"Suck eggs," Dr Beale offered, and she laughed easily.

"Since art and paint are unfamiliar to me, please let me know when I am stating the obvious," Nadezhda Bellman said, with an easy smile.

"As long as you don't mind us stopping you when the science gets beyond us," Beech said.

"I think we'll get on well," she answered. "I should add that our report was complete last week when Sir John couriered a copy of the Courtauld report to us. We've all read it and made notes that we'll relay at the end. However, we made no changes to our report after receiving it."

The presentations took nearly two hours, which I have condensed and, hopefully, made more comprehendible. Predictably, it began by describing the painting and what it appeared to be. Rather than name a painter, or a period, it was simply described by the woolly term, "antique."

Nadezhda then handed over to Dr Carrel. His French accent was strong, but his English was nuanced and witty.

"The canvas is linen and consistent with that grown and used in Northern Europe in the seventeenth and eighteenth centuries," he said.

I think we noticeably perked up as the speakers smiled, and Dr Carrel made a dampening gesture to curb our enthusiasm.

"I had to make some phone calls to confirm my memory, but painters, like Rembrandt, used a variety of canvases – coarse and fine – and that the selection had little to do with the size of the painting.

"The wood of the stretcher and member are of clear pine, also consistent with the period, and appear to be original.

"The canvas is in very good condition that suggest it experienced infrequent changes in heat and humidity," he continued. "The very minor woodworm damage suggests it was in a climate warmer and dryer than the Netherlands – or England."

This earned a chuckle.

"Dust and pollen – the details are in the report – suggest a short time in Northern France, the Netherlands or Belgium, and a prolonged period in Spain or Portugal. There are also more recent indications of pollution from wood, coal and oil smoke as well as tobacco," he said. "I also found what, for brevity, I will call 'city dust.'

"Given the pollen profiles, I'd guess that the picture went to North America around eighteen hundred to eighteen thirty. I would guess somewhere with a climate like parts of Mexico, Florida or California."

We were all nodding, and it occurred that a good theatrical 'cold reader' could contribute to the rest of the presentations.

"There was one other finding that didn't make sense to me," Dr Carrel added. "There was a large quantity of very fine paint dust.

"This was curious and I had Nadezhda test it," he said, pausing for dramatic effect. "I had supposed that the painting might have been in a workshop where it was exposed to sanding painted wood. Perhaps a place for refinishing. It's not the sort of painting to have been hung there.

"Nadezhda's findings added confusion to the picture because the paint dust corresponds to the age and type used in the period of the canvas and stretcher."

While Hawsley and Beech looked puzzled, I had a sudden realisation that neatly explained the painting Sophie had seen in *Devonshire Street* and established it as the structure of the painting before us.

"I did warn Nadezhda that this bit would pre-empt her findings," Dr Carrel said, "But, she kindly agreed that I could include it in mine.

"While carbon dating becomes less accurate the closer to the present the object tested is, both the wood and canvas were consistent in registering a timeframe of 1700 to 1725."

It took a moment for the full significance of what was said to register. Regardless of the findings of the others, the Rembrandt was definitely a forgery.

Nadezhda smiled as we glanced at each other and nodded with smug satisfaction.

"Let me give you the chemical headlines," she said. "Then Dr Beale can tell you how it was done.

"Most of the colours in the visible painting have been available for about two hundred years. The pigments in the dust Jean referred to were about a hundred years older.

"While the colour pigments have been available, they have been diluted with modern chemicals to make them flow through an inkjet printing device. There are also bulking agents, additives to create *impasto* – texture and the impression of brushstrokes – and then there are chemical markers, but we don't know what for."

"We can help you there, Miss Bellman," Hawsley said. "We believe that they trigger certain responses when detected in the standard automated computerised analytical databases."

"And sending back false readings?!" Dr Beale interjected, in terrible recognition. "That's terrible! It also explains what they were for. We couldn't guess."

"If science had a concept of evil, that would be it," Dr Carrel said.

They looked at each other with a mix of shock, but also the satisfaction in having the explanation to a puzzle.

"It was Chief Inspector Beech who put us onto that," I said. "There was another report besides the Courtauld's. It's chemical analysis was identical to the Courtauld's – to the second decimal point."

Miss Bellman was enjoying this new information.

"Jonathan, why don't you tell us what you found, then perhaps we can discuss this openly and fill in the gaps in our mutual knowledge."

Dr Beale told us that he had compared the scans of Rembrandt paintings with ones from *Storm 2*.

"The brushstrokes are well duplicated, but there is also some clever imaging."

He pushed some buttons and the lights went out and a projected image of the painting appeared on an adjacent screen.

He zoomed in.

"Look at this wave."

A red box appeared around it.

"Now, this one."

It was the same, only larger.

"And this one."

Now smaller.

"This repetition gives continuity to the overall image," he said. "Now, look at this."

The image of the wave suddenly flipped to a mirror image.

"We can see this wave here, here, and here, in different sizes."

Three areas appeared in red boxes.

"This creates the choppiness of the water," he said. "Or, at least it does to my untrained eye."

"Quite so," Hawsley said.

"We can also find it in anamorphic distortions," Dr Beale continued.

He showed us the basic wave in a red box, then distorted it by pulling on its lower left corner.

"We can see that here, and mirrored here," he said. "It's very clever and creates the desired scene of the chaotic sea but with optical tricks that unify it."

After a moment, Hawsley spoke.

"It's what composers do," he said. "They take the melody, reverse it, invert it, reverse the inversion, take it in and out of major and minor, change keys, speed it up, slow it down and then put it back together."

"Exactly," Dr Beale said.

"Since this would have been 'painted' on an X-Y printer, the mathematics of doing those things would be relatively simple," I said.

All three scientists looked surprised.

"Sir Nigel is not only a portrait painter," Beech said to them, "but a doctor of mathematics who taught at Cambridge."

Their eyes widened.

"And a fellow of the Royal Society," Hawsley added.

After a moment, Miss Bellman summarised.

"The base structure is early eighteenth century. On it we found the remains of a painting that was identified as a copy of *Belshazzar's Feast*, by Rembrandt. It is a safe assumption that the paint dust found by Dr Carrel was from scraping or sanding that down.

"The pigments you see – though available in the nineteenth century – are modern and adulterated to create the effects we've discussed. Some of these additives date from the second half of the twentieth century, but there are also some not available until the last decade."

Beech was right. The picture was newer than I had suspected.

Hawsley had moved to the back of the room and was on his mobile phone. Beech and I were leafing through the reports Miss Bellman had given us.

Hawsley rejoined us.

"Miss Bellman suggested we have a discussion about these findings and what we know," he said. "May I suggest that we do it over lunch?"

So we adjourned to a private dining room at the club and filled them in on the whole story.

Chapter XXVII

Watching the young academics enter the club on Mount Street Gardens was entertaining. Dr Carrel, being French, was used to moving easily in and out of great buildings. To a lesser extent, Nadezhda was not uncomfortable. It was the Englishman, Dr Beale, who was the least comfortable. He didn't say anything, but his body language closed up, and he became silent.

Hawsley had requested a private room. It had a round table, and once seated, even Dr Beale relaxed a little. Beech seemed to notice Beale's unease and, being seated closer to him, struck up a conversation. I was seated between Dr Carrel and Hawsley, and nearly facing Miss Bellman.

Somehow, between Hawsley's phone call and our arrival, the dining room had printed a special abbreviated menu with three starters, three *entrées* and two desserts which they handed to us.

Jean Carrel asked what I recommended, then chose something else. Dr Beale appeared comfortable with the menu and Nadezhda was so busy talking to Hawsley that she didn't look at it until the waiter asked what she wanted.

Conversation which had been hesitant at the beginning became more animated and by the time we were served, had become enthusiastically vocal.

Beech was grilling Dr Beale about imaging and how, based on his work with the "Rembrandt," the latest techniques could be applied to art. Jean was telling me about techniques to refine carbon dating, and Nadezhda was challenging Hawsley about art valuations.

It felt like one of those gatherings that could go on forever with good food, drink and fascinating conversation, but shortly after coffee, the three scientists claimed that work was calling and excused themselves.

Hawsley asked for more coffee and whisky.

"We have some work to do, but most of it is to place this mess into someone else's hands," Beech said. "I look forward to reading the report. The presentation was comprehensive, but we still need to look for other anomalies."

"I shall contact the other houses and galleries to alert them to what looks like a serious international fraud operation," Hawsley said. "I also need to coordinate a press statement. Beech, you will, no doubt, be contacting the Yard."

Beech nodded.

"And Nigel, all you have to do is keep your mouth shut," Hawsley added, with a laugh. "You may fill in Miss Gordon enough to satisfy her curiosity."

We drank our coffee and enjoyed the whisky.

"There's one question I expected you to ask," I said to Beech. "I thought you'd ask if they knew anyone who could do such work."

Beech smiled.

"Believe me, I wanted to," he replied. "However, I thought it would get better results if three detectives showed up and scared the shit out of them first."

Hawsley and I laughed.

"A shame to do it to such nice young people," he said, "but necessary and effective. They will certainly know who is at the top of their fields."

We talked about various points in the presentations and decided that whoever had advised Hawsley in choosing Nadezhda to lead the tests knew what he was doing.

"Please read the report carefully," Hawsley said, as we neared the point of having to do some work. "Let me have your notes and we can arrange a final discussion. James, I expect you will alert the unit immediately and then fill them in on anything else you find."

"After I read the report, I shall give it to them and return to my rustication," he replied.

"I don't know what, if any conclusions we can come to about people who know paintings versus computers, but once this gets out, the press will manage something,"

Hawsley said. "It's been a nerve-wracking but fascinating interruption to normal life."

Beech and I left the club together while Hawsley had stopped to talk to some friends at the bar.

"For scientists, they were remarkably personable," Beech said, with a grin, "I just hope their science is good or there will be hell to pay."

"You doubt the results?"

"I doubt their credibility," he said. "I have no doubt that they are correct in their findings, but the results are not going to sell themselves."

I considered this.

Beech looked at his watch.

"Have you got time now?" he asked.

"Where do you want to go?"

"We can go to the East India Club," he said. "You and Hawsley aren't the only ones who belong to London clubs."

ℰ

It was less than a mile to St James's Square, and the fresh air and movement were welcome. The East India Club was one of the less formal London clubs but it still did things right without being stuffy.

"I try to get here at least several times a month, but retirement is busier than most people think," Beech said. "Dora likes its friendliness and unintimidating menus."

I knew many members and had thought of joining myself as it was on one of my regular routes to my studio.

We went into the Waterloo Room, and Beech, after talking to a few friends, ordered tea. There were enough people in the room to create background noise that would make being overheard unlikely.

"You may not feel this, but I have found that once I retired, the speed at which I forget things accelerates," he said. "My initial reluctance to get involved in this enterprise stems from my desire not to bungle it.

"I've only been retired two years, but I find it hard to name the top ten forgers and art thieves currently at work," he continued. "Not only that, but many of my contacts have also retired, moved to different posts, or had the bad manners to die."

"I don't think anyone could question your contribution," I said.

Beech smiled and nodded his thanks.

"That's kind, but I failed to come up with two basic parts of a crime," he said.

While I waited for him to continue, our tea arrived.

"I have come up with no motive and not a single suspect," he said.

"But that's not why you were brought in," I replied. "Hawsley and I were looking for someone who could confirm or refute our misgivings – and you did. You were also the one to recognise that the two chemical analyses were suspiciously identical. As far as we're concerned, you delivered on your brief – and then some."

Beech smiled, drank some tea and ate a biscuit. He waited before speaking again, and when he did, his tone was more grave.

"I have the feeling that what looks straight-forward to us, now and here, untouched by the consequences of this whole business, is not as black and white as it seems," he said.

"I'd love to see the other suspect paintings," he continued. "If they are of the quality of the Rembrandt, we could be on the brink of a new Renaissance – or at least a revolution.

"Imagine taking a really good photograph – landscape or portrait – and giving it the sort of treatment that we've seen in *The Storm on the Sea of Galilee*," he said, with growing enthusiasm. "The first thing that would happen is that the silly NFTs would lose their idiotic values."

I laughed. NFTs (non-fungible tokens) weren't considered art by a lot of people. (These constituted a larger number than those who don't consider photography art.) All one owns is a certificate of ownership. The actual NFT is somewhere else and owners of NFTs have no rights whatever to the image that is on the digital file. There is no intrinsic value to them and they are no more unique than owning a five pound note

– because that, too, has a serial number that makes it unique. Vapourware and nothing more.

A.I.-generated art was another thing. We already have over-priced wide-format inkjet prints given the tarted up name of *giclée* so that more can be charged for it. There are also limited edition *giclées* printed on canvas and stretched that have finishing touches added to them by the artist, but at least the origins of these met the conventional definition of art.

All these new techniques blur the boundaries between art and mechanical reproduction. The fact remains that prints – no matter how made or by whom – have never been worth as much as the original works.

"Here's one for you," Beech said, cutting into my thoughts. "Do you know the story about Cocteau and Picasso?"

I shook my head.

"Jean Cocteau visited Picasso in his studio. Picasso was experimenting with a new subject, technique, or style. As Picasso painted, Cocteau flipped through the canvases stacked along the wall.

"The pictures appealed to Cocteau, and when he got back to his studio, he painted one in that style, as an experiment," Beech related, engagingly.

"Some time later, Picasso visited Cocteau and similarly rooted through the stack of pictures in Cocteau's studio and found the copy of his work.

"'I don't remember giving you this,' Picasso said.

"'You didn't. I painted it.'

"After arguing about it for a while, Picasso shouts, 'Bollocks! It's one of mine!' and he grabs one of Cocteau's brushes and signs it."

We were both laughing by the time he reached the end of the anecdote, then he looked directly at me and asked:

"Is it a Picasso or a fake?"

All I could do was laugh and shrug.

"It's a joke," I said.

"It's a true story," Beech said.

"No, the *painting* is a joke."

"Picasso didn't think so."

I thought a moment.

"And that's where you think we're headed?" I asked.

"I think that for too long people who should know better have been more concerned with *who* did something rather than *what* was done.

"I'm talking about art here," Beech added, hurriedly, "not bank robbery."

I laughed, but he was serious.

"I'm a cop. I try to catch people who break the law. It doesn't matter if I don't like the law, or personally feel that what was done should have been done. I can vote and write to my M.P. like everyone else," he said, "but to my simple mind, that Rembrandt of ours deserves to be seen and who – or what – painted it doesn't matter."

I considered this.

"Are you comfortable with that?"

Beech gave another of his ironic smiles.

"Does it matter if I am?" he asked, but he continued before I could object. "No, I'm not comfortable with it, and it does matter to me, but what can I do?

"In my career, I saw the ugly part of the art world – the greed, corruption, the cheating and theft. I've seen my share of vandalism, too."

This was the first time I had any insight into Beech's values or personal regard for art.

"Let me ask you, would you really be happy to see our fake Rembrandt destroyed? That's what they sometimes do with fakes: they are ordered destroyed. Beautiful things; they just don't have the right name.

"This is the law at its most existential. What condemns the work – and the person who painted it – is the *intention to deceive*. The work itself has done nothing except to bring pleasure, and then embarrassment and then anger, and so it must be destroyed."

"Do we want skill, originality or authenticity?" I asked.

Beech thought a moment.

"That, too, appears to be shifting ground," he said. "By accident, back in the 1980s, I got to know the chap who sold Royal Doulton China in Asia.

"The Japanese, like the Americans, have a great affection for royalty, and British goods with a Royal Warrant are particularly desirable there," he said.

"The salesman told me that this was one of his best markets in the East and the Japanese loved it in spite of its flaws, his major buyer said.

"'Flaws!?' the salesman exclaimed. The buyer showed him a plate with the slightest irregularity in the silver ring that ran around the edge," Beech continued. "The salesman explained that these were hardly flaws, but signs that they had been hand-painted. Apparently, the Japanese are used to perfection in such things because it is all done by machine.

"I think we are approaching similar attitudes in art," he said.

As one who always looks for the deliberate flaws in oriental rugs, I found the idea of mechanically perfect art unattractive, but then, I'd never seen any.

"The art world isn't a sleeping tiger, but it may be a basking serpent," Beech said, finishing his tea.

"Nemo me impune lacessit," I said.

"Indeed."

Chapter XXVIII

I glanced at my watch when I left the East India Club. If I went back to my rooms, Sophie would come around for a drink and want to talk. There was too much to digest before talking to her, so I went to the Royal Academy. The exhibition galleries were closed, but the Keeper's House was open and I found a seat and began reading the Imperial report. For form, I bought a sparkling water, but I'd been drinking all afternoon.

The presentation had covered all the salient points and other information had come out over lunch. The report was well organised and clearly written. I was impressed because it stuck to the scientific and did not stray into commenting on the work itself, apart from noting the presence of *Belshazzar's Feast* in the X-rays which someone had taken the trouble to identify.

Beech had seemed to suggest that our discoveries would not be acted on – or appreciated.

I stopped my reading and began making notes on what Beech had said: The Rembrandt, the Royal Doulton's imperfections, and the amusing tale of Picasso and Cocteau.

What it came down to was the question, "Where does value lie?"

Most of this flew in the face of my Augustinian Platonism and embraced the worst sort of relativism. I had to recognise that that was reality, and things had been that way for some time.

Even Michelangelo was a forger in his youth, but his forgeries – if recognised – are now worth far more than the originals he forged.

Other artists regularly distorted the truth, too. Many portraits ignore the scars of syphilis or smallpox, Victorian cityscapes are sanitised and romanticised, and as anyone who has tried it knows, aligning the Venetian towers and buildings with a Canaletto is an exercise in futility. Even I am guilty of giving face lifts, removing blemishes, or enhancing a figure – but that is what art is, a selective representation.

Photographs were heralded as new proofs of truth but they very quickly became as unreliable and dishonest as art. Yet, great art – and maybe even good art – has a rightness that speaks to the soul.

Perhaps Sophie is right, and it is possible to over-think things.

When Bunyan wrote, "all was vanity and vexation of spirit, and there was no profit under the sun," he clearly had no concept of a London auction house.

৪৩

It was nearly six when I got back to Albany. Sophie gave me twenty minutes before she tapped on my door and entered.

"Just back from your boozy lunch?" she asked.

I called to her from the bedroom and told her to make us drinks and that I'd be with her shortly.

I found her reading, drink in hand.

"Tell me all about it," she said, closing the magazine.

There wasn't much I couldn't tell her, though I spared her my ethical digressions. She was particularly concerned that someone would destroy an early eighteenth century copy of *Belshazzar's Feast* to put a fake Rembrandt on top of it.

"We don't value copies today," I said. "That's a pity. The casts of classical sculpture in the V&A are a good example. For more than a hundred years, they barely got a look. Once photography and cinema became popular, people thought, why look at a copy? It's worse today with the web. We can get hundreds of images and views of the most obscure objects.

"Only recently, has it been recognised that the detail on the plaster casts of classical sculpture is better than the detail on the originals which have deteriorated in a century of air pollution," I said. "The same can be true of paintings."

Sophie nodded.

"I hadn't thought of that. It was the way we used to know great art and architecture," she said. "My school had a plaster scale model of the Parthenon gathering dust on a top shelf. We never looked at it – just at colour photographs and films."

"You've seen the copy of *The Last Supper* at the R.A.?" I asked.

"The huge one? Yes, of course."

"It was painted in about 1525, shortly after Da Vinci's death, probably by one of his students," I said. "For years, it hung behind a false wall in one of the galleries until it was uncovered and cleaned in the 1980s. It gives us a very good idea of what Da Vinci's looked like when new. It even shows Christ's feet, which were lost when a door was put into the refectory in the seventeenth century. The details were so good, it was used in the restoration of the original."

Sophie smiled and thought for a moment.

"I can never think of that painting without thinking of the joke, 'Sit on this side if you want to get in the picture.' It's a strange composition having everyone on the same side of the table."

I laughed.

"Artistically and literally, it is," I agreed. "But remember, it was the refectory of Dominican nuns, so the idea was Christ was at the high table and they were seated with Him and the apostles at their real meals."

"That's quite a thought."

"It is, but it probably didn't stop cattiness and bad behaviour."

Sophie laughed.

"So, is that the end of your great forgery adventure?" she asked.

"Probably for me and Beech," I answered. "Hawsley will coordinate things for a while, but I expect Scotland Yard, Europol and whoever looks after such things in South Africa, South America and the United States will be picking it up," I said. "There are not many people who can tell a really good forgery from the real thing. I think a lot of it is unconscious observation that the brain flags up. Also, you have to be able to divorce yourself from all prejudices – which is impossible for most people."

When we finished our drinks, we went out and wandered towards Shepherd Market and found a noisy Japanese restaurant. Sophie was a fan, and, as long as I didn't have to eat sushi, I was content.

We spent longer than usual over dinner. Sophie talked about some possible new projects. She was always in demand, but she found choosing new productions increasingly difficult.

"It's so hard not to get typecast these days," she complained. "Producers who typecast actors can slash their marketing budgets. 'If it's so-and-so, then it's a thriller.' That's what's wonderful about RSC training.

They're taught that acting is a job and you simply do it. Comfort zone doesn't enter into it. I'm sorry I missed that experience. By all accounts it was gruelling, but few RSC actors get typecast without their complicity."

"When does the Stoppard open?" I asked.

"At the beginning of July," she said. "My contract is for a year, but it can be renewed or cut. After that, there's talk of playing Gertrude for a new production at the National in two years, but they're trying to get the BBC to buy into it."

"I'm surprised you haven't done *Great Celebrity Bake Off*," I said.

She laughed loudly.

"When have you eaten anything I've baked?" she challenged.

"My birthday cake last year was delicious."

She looked down and went quiet.

"Sophie?"

She twisted her napkin like a little girl.

"I bought it," she whispered.

"You what?! I'm sure you told me you made it."

"I bought it," she repeated, daring to look up. "From those nice men across the street. I asked them for an un-iced cake, then bought a tin of butter icing."

She looked down again, but I suspected she was giggling.

"Nice men across the street?"

"Bill and Hugh."

I made an exaggerated expression.

"William Fortnum and Hugh Mason," I sighed. "Oh, Sophie! And to think I thought I saw a glimmer of domesticity."

We walked back to Albany. It was the warmest evening of the year, so we took our time, stopping to look in windows.

I was feeling relaxed and good about the world for pretty much the first time that day. I was also pleased that discussion about Marissa had been avoided.

"Do you want a coffee?" she asked.

"I'd better go up," I said, wanting to maintain a Marissa-free evening. "I want to make an early start and make sure all's ready for April. You *are* coming, aren't you?"

"I'll see you at ten-thirty."

"Don't fail me. I have no idea what to expect after Marissa's performance."

Back in my study, I continued reading Nadezhda's report and compared the charts to the ones from California. As she'd said, the chemistry was completely different. That the California results so exactly matched the Courtauld's could only indicate a tampering with the database. Collusion was out of the question.

It would be interesting to see how the rest of this incident played out. Would there be more paintings before the perpetrators were rounded up?

I doubted that Hawsley fully appreciated how he had preserved the integrity of the art market.

Chapter XXIX

The studio was set up exactly as it had been when I unveiled Marissa's portrait for her, and later, for Sophie. I didn't have champagne, but there was tea and coffee, some biscuits (courtesy of Bill and Hugh), and sherry in the event that April lingered. I hoped she'd be gone so Sophie and I could go to lunch.

The rest of my day would be free, but the painting would begin again on Wednesday.

There had been a good deal of rearranging to accommodate the various "Rembrandt Meetings," as Sophie called them. I didn't like messing clients about, but Sophie told me to tell them that I was obliged to postpone their sitting because, "I had been commanded to be elsewhere at a place I was not allowed to name."

I don't like lying, but Sophie said that this kept explanations short, made the customer feel he was being painted by someone even more distinguished than he'd thought, and made them feel good about being inconvenienced by – well, whoever they thought was commanding me.

Vanity, vanity.

Sophie arrived at ten-thirty, as promised, and brought another bunch of flowers. These were long ones with clusters of blossoms along the length. (Portrait painters don't need to know the names of all the plants, flowers, fruit and veg that still life painters need to know.)

She put her coat in the bedroom and found a vase, filled it and arranged the flowers as she had done before.

"One would think your design sense comes from the Cistercians," she said, as she tweaked the curtains. "Your chambers are just the same."

I had adjusted my studio lighting to highlight Marissa's portrait, and it intensified the effect of the dark blue velvet drape.

"Have we got time for – "

Sophie's question was interrupted by the intercom. I said good morning, gave April the floor number and buzzed her in.

I put the kettle on and Sophie went onto the landing to meet her.

Both were making more noise than usual when they entered the studio, but it was mostly laughter.

April looked like she was going from Bickering Place to the petrol station rather than to London. She wore a tweed skirt, low, soft rubber-soled lace-up shoes, a lavender jumper and a Barbour.

"At least she wasn't wearing a headscarf or someone might have mistaken her for the Queen," Sophie later said.

She asked for tea. Sophie and I had coffee. We sat chatting easily – well, April and Sophie chatted as I listened.

April talked of the weather, the train journey, the Underground and how Marissa's directions had been perfect.

"Is that it?" she asked, breaking off pointing, pretending that the one metre square form on an easel, covered with a midnight blue piece of velvet and illuminated with sophisticated lighting had escaped her notice.

"It is," I said. "Would you like to see it now?"

April thought a moment.

"Let's catch up first," she said. "Prolong the suspense."

She turned to Sophie.

"I can't tell you how Marissa talked about it. She can't wait to get it home," April said, reaching for another biscuit. "She said that although she'd seen it from the start, seeing the finished picture was a revelation."

"It is exciting, isn't it?" Sophie said. "I know just what she means."

"I envy her the experience," April said. "There's something intimate about being painted, and one never knows what it might lead to."

"Would you like some more tea, April?" I asked, hoping to divert this train of thought onto a siding.

"That would be lovely, Sir Nigel."

I glanced at Sophie as I took her mug, but she didn't meet my eye.

As I made April her tea, I listened to her tell Sophie about my time at Bickering Place. There was no mention of Marissa's reluctance, her initial indifference to the project, or her failure to show up on time.

April did have some interesting – if curious – comments about our relationship.

"I could tell that things were going well when she so easily called him, 'Nigel'," she said. "I was rather shocked at first, but once I realised how close they had become, I could see how understandable it was."

Somehow I managed to deliver the tea and coffee without spilling – or throwing – it.

April stopped talking long enough to take a sip, and I decided to move things along.

"Shall we have a look now?" I asked, moving towards the easel.

Sophie put her coffee down and took April's cup and saucer from her and set it down on the table.

They moved to about three feet from the canvas, and I removed the drape.

I watched April's face carefully. Her eyes moved to various parts of the painting and returned to Marissa's face after each look elsewhere.

I looked at Sophie who was beginning to appear concerned and continued watching April.

"I could start talking to her," she finally said, with a big grin. "It's just like going into the hallway."

I stepped back, content that the portrait was in no danger. Sophie caught my eye and visibly relaxed.

"I wish she'd dressed like that more," April said, turning to Sophie. "Perhaps she will now that she's obviously so happy."

April returned to the sofa, picked up her tea and continued to look.

"As I said to Marissa, I'd like to submit this to the Summer Exhibition," I said. "You both can come see it, and at the end of August, I can send it up to you."

"It would be exciting to see this in an exhibition," April said. "But you must bring it yourself and stay. You can advise us where to hang it."

I smiled at her.

"I can do that right now," I said.

I stood and went back to the painting.

"This wall to the right of the window, where the mirror is, behind the flowers, is big enough," I said. "It could be seen by all your visitors."

April approached the portrait again and suddenly clapped her hands.

"That would be splendid!" she exclaimed. "You know, you could paint it there now! That would be amusing."

She returned to the sofa.

"I see why Marissa was so excited by this," she said. "It's wonderful that you could see what she's really like so quickly."

She turned to Sophie.

"It shows how well they connected," she continued. "Marissa was totally relaxed with him. I don't know what he did, but I could see it whenever they were together. Do you know," she leaned confidentially toward Sophie, "that she even changed her clothes in front of him – and me."

She looked at me to confirm the anecdote. I think I was powerless to react at all, but Sophie covered her mouth, her eyes wide.

April stood and retrieved her Barbour from the bedroom and put it on.

"It's just wonderful for a mother to finally see," she said, looking at me and patting my arm. "I want you to know that whatever you two decide to do is fine with me!"

It was the sound of the door closing that snapped Sophie and me back to reality.

"*Go!*" I said sharply to Sophie, grabbing her coat from the bedroom and holding it out to her. "Find out what the hell she thinks is going on!"

I continued to hold the coat out, but Sophie hadn't budged from the sofa.

"What's the matter with you?!" I snapped. "Go! I can't have her going back to Lincolnshire thinking – *that!*"

I was exasperated by Sophie's lack of movement, and then she burst into nearly uncontrolled laughter. I sputtered and fussed, but she only laughed harder until she had to find some tissues in her handbag to dry her eyes.

I sat down and slumped in my armchair.

"You didn't tell me you had that much fun in Lincolnshire," Sophie said, wiping her eyes and continuing to giggle. "Have you picked out a ring yet? It sounds like it's a wonder you got any painting done."

I suppose it was good that Sophie didn't take it seriously. She drank her coffee and continued to chuckle intermittently. I'd think she had regained her composure, then she'd look at me and collapse again.

"Isn't it nice being thought attractive by a girl young enough to be your granddaughter?" she teased.

"It might be, but Marissa Gilliat had very little time for me," I said. "Getting any input from her was like pulling teeth."

Sophie gave me one of her signature looks that I'd seen in her films and on television for decades. It still had the same fresh look and the power to disarm.

"Poor Nigel," she mocked.

I scoffed, but it, too, was mocking.

I gave a long sigh.

"Come, I'll take you to lunch," she said, "but you have to tell me about Marissa undressing."

I didn't rise to the bait. I took Marissa's portrait from the easel, slid it into the storage rack, and switched off the lights.

I was holding the door open when the telephone rang.

I started to ignore it, but it could have been a client wanting to reschedule a sitting.

"I'd better take it," I said apologetically to Sophie.

It was Hawsley.

"Can you come to my office right now?" he said, after saying hello.

I told him I was on my way to lunch with Sophie.

"She'll understand when you tell her," he said, abruptly. "There's a major high impact shit-fan interface about to happen."

"And I can stop it?"

Hawsley never took his old-fashioned dictatorial tone with me. Indeed, he appeared to seldom use it with anyone.

"No," he said, more normally. "No one can, but I'd appreciate advice from an old friend about how to deal with it."

After hanging up, I looked at Sophie, raised my eyebrows and shrugged.

"You owe me dinner," she said.

Chapter XXX

B rooke & Sons was in a row of purple brick townhouses in Dover Street. Over the years, buildings and rooms had been knocked together to create a comfortable salesroom and a number of preview rooms. Much of this space had originally been courtyards and service alleys. One of the consequences of these renovations was that the administrative offices were pushed either to the upper floors or into the cellars.

Works under assessment or being considered for future sales were stored across the river in secure warehouses.

Hawsley's office was on the third floor, and had three long Westward-facing windows, giving excellent light. While the ceilings weren't as high as on the lower floors, they were still over eight-feet and gave a sense of spacious accommodation.

I'd only been there a few times, but it appeared to have changed little.

At one end of the rectangular room was Hawsley's antique desk, and at the other end was a large, equally old bookcase filled with reference books and sale catalogues. Occupying most of the room was a boardroom table that could seat twelve comfortably.

It was of an oriental style with black lacquer *zhuo* legs and in-turned feet. The top had a black lacquer border that framed a burl walnut veneered top that reflected a central brass chandelier.

On closer inspection, various bits of electronic kit could be seen. A mini-projector peaked out of the top of the bookcase and a retractable screen was neatly tucked into the plaster moulding above Hawsley's desk.

There were also two leather armchairs and a low table with copies of the latest *Burlington*, *Apollo* and *Spectator* magazines.

"Thank you for coming at short notice, and please extend my apologies to Miss Gordon," he said, warmly.

He looked worried, and I thought even shaken.

"I will take you both to dinner when the dust settles. You deserve a reward for your help, tolerance and patience."

We sat in the leather armchairs. He turned his to face me better, and I reciprocated.

"When I left Imperial, I was in an excellent mood," he began. "Our connoisseurship had uncovered one forgery and probably a major international fraud. I was full of admiration for everyone – Beech, you, and the clever people at Imperial.

"At the same time, my head was spinning as to what to do next. Beech would hand everything over to Scotland

Yard, and I had to deal with the owners, galleries and auction houses."

He paused, and it led me to think he'd been up all night.

"I wrote down the names of all involved, where they were and how many hours different they were to London."

"An all nighter?"

He nodded.

"There was no question that the first person to talk to was Helena Stirakis. The Courtauld needed to be protected," he said, with gravitas. "I called her and caught her just as she was leaving. I persuaded her to come here as fast as she could.

"She was expecting some sort of serious news when she arrived, but not that I'd had the audacity to have her work double-checked."

"I had our repro department make a colour copy of the Imperial report for her," he said, and drew his hand over his face as if to wipe away the memory.

Then, he smiled.

"I'm sorry, Nigel. This will only take about fifteen minutes and then we can go to the club for a few stiff drinks and a late lunch.

"I suppose I expected Helena to be grateful to learn that the shared database was corrupted, but her reaction was rather different," he said.

Hawsley told me, in great, painful detail, that the lovely Dr Stirakis had been furious that we should a) question their expertise, b) trust people who knew nothing about art, and c) keep her out of the loop. It hadn't been until he told her that the Yard and Europol would be investigating that she began to see the bigger picture.

"However," he continued, "this morning, she called to thank me and say that steps were underway to withdraw the report and address the database issues, but by then, there had been a tectonic shift."

"A result, then," I said, encouragingly.

Hawsley shook his head.

"Only partially," he said. "After Helena left, I called Weisman & Rossi in Los Angeles. They reminded me they'd had their own tests done, and that they would be standing by their assessment.

"To them it was demonstrably a Rembrandt. I made several attempts to tell them that there was adequate evidence to prove it was a fake. When that didn't work, I raised the possibility that when it was proven to be a forgery, they could be cited as complicit."

This level of "persuasion" was extreme, but justifiable.

"And?"

"They hung up."

"They had pointed out that there were three reports, two of which concluded that the landscape version of *The*

Storm on the Sea of Galilee was genuine, and the dissenting report was by individuals of no standing in the art world."

"But all you have to do is look!" I protested.

"But who will?" Hawsley replied. "It's in no one's interest."

I was speechless.

"I tried to contact Helena until nearly midnight, but couldn't reach her. I had to give her the bad news this morning when she called to say she'd come around to understanding," he said, ruefully. "I'm afraid I ruined her day."

"What about the others?"

"I spoke to the Rijksmuseum this morning. They told me they were content with the Steen, but had not yet made up their mind to buy it."

"Did they test it again, or rely on the report from Gwilym Jones & Stottlemeyer?"

"They didn't say, which means they didn't."

"And the others?" I asked.

"They were very polite, thanked me for the heads-up and pointed out that only their tests were being run on the other recently discovered works," he said. "By the time I was two thirds of the way down the list, it was clear that they'd all been in touch with each other. By the time I got to the Wildenstein, they declined to talk to me.

"Everyone was polite, but uninterested, and won't be pursuing the matter," he said.

"I gather that means they're going to sell them as genuine, or open a *musée des faux arts*."

Hawsley glared at me but nodded.

"They might fudge the attribution of the Old Masters, 'After Steen', 'Circle of Rembrandt', 'Attributed to Thomas Lawrence'. . . . Well, they might be detected one day after evidence that someone in the art world acknowledges comes to light and the villains caught, but in the meantime, we're powerless."

"And the Art and Antiquities Unit?" I asked.

"Well, they may do something, but if the Rembrandt leaves Britain – and without an owner or agent filing a complaint – it won't be a top priority."

Hawsley was as infuriated as I, but he'd had time to assess the situation and accept reality.

೧೪

We were silent as we left the building and made our way to Mount Street Gardens.

Apart from greeting friends at the club, we remained quiet until half-way through our second gin and tonic.

"I think it's time I retired," Hawsley said.

I laughed, not taking him seriously.

"There's only so much you can turn a blind eye to," he said. "More and more of these forgeries will appear, and people will be happy to pay millions for them. The technology will get better and better.

"Let's face it, that Rembrandt is a cracker!" he suddenly exclaimed. "As a dramatic thing of beauty and technical achievement – human or mechanical – it's a fantastic piece. It was hard not to believe it was the real thing."

"Who would dare to hang it?" I challenged.

"Private collectors. Some galleries – after all, a bit of controversy can be good for a museum or gallery," he said, with an impish smile. "Some have estimated that twenty percent of the art in museums is either fake or misattributed – and the misattributions go both ways.

"When Everett Fahy of the Metropolitan – the museum in New York, not the police force – identified Francesco Granacci's *St John the Baptist Bearing Witness* as being by Michelangelo, its estimated value went from a few hundred thousand to several hundred million.

"But what does it matter?" he asked, reflectively. "The National Gallery in Washington isn't going to sell it. All it really does is gain some kudos for Fahy and the museum and put up insurance and security costs. It's a free museum, so there's no benefit from increased visitor numbers. There are too many other examples."

"And the next generation of curators will question those judgements, too," I said. "But does any of this get us nearer the truth?"

"Truth?" Hawsley pondered.

Narcissism, I thought.

Hawsley stared into space for a moment.

"What makes me think it's time to go is that I realised that no one wanted to hear what I was telling them," he made a dismissive sound. "That's just vanity – which is another good reason to retire."

"You're not sixty yet," I protested. "What would you do?"

He smiled.

"I had the idea of putting together an art verification company that did all its chemical analysis the old-fashioned way," he said. "Anything that required a computer would be air-gapped."

"That's a brilliant idea," I said, enthusiastically.

"I thought so, too, until I realised I'd never get any customers," he said. "People would rather believe in dreams. Now, let's get some lunch."

Epilogue

When Sophie came round in the evening, I cooked her a sea bass. It was one of her favourite things. She liked it better than shellfish, so I took the opportunity of preparing some scallops for myself – though she stole a few of them, too.

She brought a bottle of something fizzy (she looked after it; I never saw the label), and asked me what was so important that I left her on her own for lunch.

Considering the events of the morning – which after my session with Hawsley, seemed to be in the distant past – Sophie was very relaxed. Unless this was her "calm-before-the-storm" act, in which case, I'd have to behave all the way through dinner.

"Hawsley said he'll take us to dinner," I said.

"I know," she said, coyly. "He dropped a note around."

"Flowers?"

"No," she said. "He knows his place."

I laughed.

"I'm not sure he does," I said. "He's talking about retiring."

Although she'd only met him a few times, Sophie was shocked.

"I thought he had international status," she said.

"He feels he's lost it now."

Over dinner, I told her what had been so urgent that he'd called me. To her, it made no sense.

"It's real or it isn't!" she exclaimed. "Does it really matter who did the testing? Shouldn't it at least be a red flag to order an investigation, or at least more tests?"

"Not if the owners or agents don't want to submit the pictures," I said. "They have a report they're satisfied with and that's it."

"And they will sell them as real?"

I explained the various attributions, then threw in the tease.

"If someone thinks it's a lovely painting, why not sell it to them. They may not care if it has a bit of controversy about it."

That was enough to keep her talking through dinner and dessert. Indeed, it carried her well into coffee, when she finally realised that it had been a tactical manoeuvre.

She put her coffee cup down.

"Sit on the sofa," she said, pointing to the other corner.

I moved and sat and turned towards her. And then she did the unexpected – nay, unprecedented – and moved over, sat down and leaned against me. I resisted the temptation to put my arm around her, as I knew she was on a knife edge and could probably not sustain the proximity for long.

"Well, I've got surprising news for you, too," she said.

ॐ

Over the course of the next year, the paintings did go on sale.

Someone in California had realised that promoting the first A.I. painted "Rembrandt" would have a market in Silicon Valley, and indeed, it did. It was regarded as an event of similar significance to Deep Blue beating Garry Kasparov. Driving up the bidding were Stanford, the University of California, Caltech and, not to be left out, MIT, Carnegie Mellon, Texas A&M and ETH Zurich.

It sold for the same price as a wholly respectable Rembrandt, illustrating why American university fees are so high.

Brooke & Sons refused to participate in the sale of any of the recently discovered paintings, and that sealed Hawsley's fate. He jumped before he was pushed.

The Holbein had been downgraded to "attributed to" Holbein, but it was enough for a successful auction. The Thomas Lawrence and the Bronzino were sold to a private buyer and a museum respectively.

Of the Steen, there was no news, but two years later, I saw it hanging in the Rijksmuseum.

Of the Modigliani: after it was sent to Paris, it was never heard of again.

At least, not yet.

Hawsley is enjoying the countryside and writes an occasional column on salmon fishing.

I learned Sophie's surprising news in June when she became Dame Ligeia Gordon, CBE.

The year had been a good one for me, too.

I exhibited Marissa's portrait at the Royal Academy Summer Exhibition where it won one of the newspaper prizes for best portrait at the show. The portrait of "Gillian," the banker, won a prize at the Royal Society of Portrait Painters' Summer Exhibition for architectural features in a portrait.

Sophie and I went to one of the Friends' Previews at the R.A. Inevitably, she was recognised, but people left her alone for the most part. Many tried to take photographs of her unobtrusively, and a few had friends take pictures of themselves with Sophie just happening to be in the shot.

We had finished our Pimms and were well into the exhibition. We had stopped in front of a large portrait by Sir Alexander Josephson (President of the Royal Academy), of the young, enigmatic heiress, Arabella Montefusco, standing in a lush, rustic garden.

Sophie was engrossed in the painting.

"It has amazing depth of field," she said. "Everything is bright and sharp. You can feel the heat of the summer's day."

There was, indeed, a Pre-Raphaelite quality about the detail, and we looked for insect life in the foliage.

"There's a ladybird!" Sophie exclaimed, excitedly, but I was distracted.

While I'd been looking, too, albeit from a bit further back than Sophie, I was aware of a woman standing fairly close to me. I paid little attention and began to step back further, but then, she took my hand.

"Marissa!" I said, loudly enough for Sophie to turn and see us.

"Hello, Nigel," she said.

Sophie abandoned the entomological expedition and came to us.

"Sophie," Marissa said, as if acknowledging an unwanted kid-sister.

"Marissa," she replied, then turned back to the painting, but not before catching my eye.

Her expression of glee was infuriating.

"Have you seen it yet?" Marissa asked. "I can't wait."

"It's in the next gallery," I said, hoping she'd run off to see it.

Of course, she didn't.

"Is this one of yours, too?" she asked, indicating the Josephson.

"You know better than to ask that," I said.

"That's right. It's not square," she said, and bit her lip.

Sophie finally took pity on me and came to my other side.

"Do you like it?" she asked Marissa, nodding towards the picture.

She considered it.

"I suppose it's nice," she said. "I told you I didn't know anything about flowers and gardens."

Ordinarily, I would have pointed out a few things, but I knew that Marissa was feigning her ignorance. Anyone who knew about the French Academic methods would be able to understand this portrait.

I began to move to other paintings in the gallery, in the hopes that Marissa wouldn't be interested.

"Is your mother here?" Sophie asked, conversationally – demonstrating what an outstanding actress she was.

"No. She said she'd seen the picture and that it would be in the house by the end of the summer."

"You've seen it too," Sophie said, innocently.

Marissa actually seemed to think before replying. She would know that I'd told Sophie about her reaction at my studio.

"I wanted to see Nigel," she said. "Seeing *me* here is a bonus."

It was my turn to look away and smirk.

Sophie was silent.

I continued to sneak off and see other pictures, but my solitude wasn't going to last. Sophie pulled my arm.

"Marissa wants to see her picture," she whispered, adding, "w*ith you*."

I had not seen the portrait since it was hung. It occupied the space to the side of the doorway to the next gallery and undoubtedly had some presence. I did not expect the crowd that stood around it. Years before, when Sophie's portrait had been exhibited, it had attracted crowds, but that was an unusual portrait of a well-known personality. This was a domestic portrait of an unknown woman.

Marissa was clearly surprised by the attention she was getting.

"Damn! I should have worn that dress," she said, as we walked towards the painting.

"Or, you could just change into it here," Sophie whispered to me.

Marissa moved carefully through the crowd. She was slightly to one side, looking carefully at the picture.

"I bet she wishes she looked that good," Sophie whispered again.

"Sophie!" I said, almost too loudly.

She pulled on my arm, stood on her toes and whispered in my ear:

"I know exactly what she's going to say next," she said.

Most of the crowd moved on without realising that they had a star – two stars – in their midst.

Marissa ran towards me.

"Come, stand with me next to the picture," she said, handing her mobile phone to Sophie.

I looked at Sophie and shrugged my shoulders.

"At last," I said, "a chance for you to be on the other side of the camera."

She stuck out her tongue as I went to stand next to Marissa.

She wanted a series of pictures: her with the picture; me with the picture; both of us on either side; both on the same side.

As the photo-shoot went on, people began to watch. It didn't take long for Marissa to be recognised as the woman in the painting. Then, someone recognised Sophie and more mobile phones came out.

Finally, I turned to Marissa to say that that was enough when she threw her arms around me and kissed me. Some people actually applauded, though I am sure they had no idea who I was.

Sophie had doggedly kept shooting pictures. If she had known that the results would be posted by Marissa that evening on social media sites and appear elsewhere over the next few weeks, she may not have been as enthusiastic. Some were picked up by newspapers and art magazines. Even the R.A.'s Friends' magazine asked for permission to print one.

While unused to such publicity, it didn't frighten me as much as what Marissa had said immediately after the pictures were taken.

She approached Sophie – who had resisted my whispered suggestion that she drop the phone – and thanked her.

"I look forward to your visit, Nigel, when you come to deliver the painting. Stay for a week," she said, laughing. "You come, too, Sophie. You can keep Mother occupied."

Afterword

The cornerstone of the art market is the knowledge, experience and integrity of those who work in it and the institutions that employ them.

Charlatans and conmen will always be with us, but the work of the institutes mentioned in this book have a pedigree of service and performance that embodies their reputation.

None of the real organisations mentioned in *Circle of Vanity* is impugned. Indeed, I thank them for helping my research.

Bibliography

Bennett, A. (1991) *A Question of Attribution*. BBC, *Screen One*, Series 3, Episode 8.

Brewer, J. (2009). *The American Leonardo.* London: Constable.

Bunyan, J. (2008). *Pilgrim's Progress*, London: Penguin Books.

Diaz, J. "So Many Museums are Filled with Fake Paintings," *Fast Company*, 1 May 2018. https://www.fastcompany.com/90170415/so-many-museums-are-filled-with-fake-paintings

Eco, U. (1995) *Faith in Fakes: Travels in Hyperreality*. London: Minerva (Mandarin Paperbacks).

Glover, M. "The Big Question: How many of the paintings in our public museums are fakes?" *The Independent*, London, 16 April 2010.

Khami, M. M. (2014). *Who Says That's Art?* New York: Pro Arte Books.

Ramsey, G. C. (1967) *Agatha Christie: Mistress of Mystery*. New York: Dodd, Mead.

Shaw, G. B. (1933), *Pygmalion*, London: Longman Group Ltd.

Stein, A-M. (1973). *Three Picassos Before Breakfast.* New York: Hawthorn Books.

Stout, R. (1964). "Murder is Corny" in *Trio for Blunt Instruments.* New York: Viking Press.

Waugh, E. (1945), *Brideshead Revisited.* London: Chapman and Hall.

Acknowledgements

Annabel Elton, commissions consultant, Royal Society of Portrait Painters

The Summer Exhibition team at the Royal Academy of Arts

Institution of Mechanical Engineers

Julie Dexter, editor, proof-reader, critic

Derrick Swain, author of *Gold Cufflinks*

Ian Thomson, novelist, teacher, literary consultant and Lancastrian.

By the same author:

The Trumbull Chronicles

Fourscore and Upward
The Time of No Horizon
In an Age without Honor

Stories

Undivulged Crimes
Thoughts and Whispers
Clubs, Bills and Partisans

Novels

Ardmore Endings
The Rock Pool
Lost Lady
On the Edge of Dreams and Nightmares
The Countess Comes Home
Entrusted in Confidence
Portland Place: A novel of the time of Jane Austen
The Camels of the Qur'an
Wachusett
Nantucket Summer

Printed in Great Britain
by Amazon